Déjà Vu, Italian Style

Lou Macaluso

PEGASUS BOOKS

Pegasus Books
3338 San Marino Ave
San Jose, CA 95127
www.pegasusbooks.net

First Edition: May 2015

Published in North America by Pegasus Books. For information, please contact Pegasus Books c/o Christopher Moebs, 3338 San Marino Ave, San Jose, CA 95127.

This book is a work of fiction. Any resemblance to actual persons, living or dead, events, or locales is entirely coincidental.

Library of Congress Cataloguing-In-Publication Data
Lou Macaluso
Déjà vu, Italian Style/Lou Macaluso– 1st ed
p. cm.
Library of Congress Control Number: 2015936170

ISBN – 978-1-941859-22-3
1. FICTION / Mystery & Detective / International Mystery & Crime. 2. FICTION / Noir. 3. FICTION / Thrillers / Suspense. 4. ARCHITECTURE / Buildings / Landmarks & Monuments 5. TRAVEL / Europe / Italy. 6. FICTION / Romance / Action & Adventure.

10 9 8 7 6 5 4 3 2 1

Comments about *Déjà Vu, Italian Style* and requests for additional copies, book club rates and author speaking appearances may be addressed to Lou Macaluso or Pegasus Books c/o Christopher Moebs, 3338 San Marino Ave, San Jose, CA, 95127, or you can send your comments and requests via e-mail to cmoebs@pegasusbooks.net.

Also available as an eBook from Internet retailers and from Pegasus Books

Printed in the United States of America

*To my wife, Dorinda,
whose love of travel and
European culture inspired
this book and my life.*

Sudden Light

I have been here before
But when or how I cannot tell:
I know the grass beyond the door,
The sweet keen smell,
The sighing sound,
The lights around the shore.

—*Dante Gabriel Rossetti (1850)*

Déjà Vu, Italian Style

INTRODUCTION

Lou Macaluso is a thief. That's right, a regular pocket-picking, purse-snatching, John Dillinger wannabe. What did he steal? I'll get to that later, although some of you more literary mystery-buff-types might have already guessed.

You see, I'm in a rather unique position to make that outrageous accusation. I'm Mick, a character that Lou created in his last Tony Morelli mystery, *In Search of Sal*. Not much chance of Lou suing me for libel; it would be like Edgar Bergen suing Charlie McCarthy, or the other way around. (You younger readers might want to Google those names to get the joke.) I don't want to say too much about myself other than I'm Tony's lifelong friend and now his business manager/literary agent. Lou and Tony have this literary rule: SHOW. DON'T TELL. (Truth is they both tend to bend or break that rule and have to be reprimanded by their editors.)

In Search of Sal was told from what Lou calls third-person-tightly-held-point-of-view. That means someone outside the story narrates it but hangs around Tony most of the time. He toyed with the idea of letting me narrate *Déjà Vu, Italian Style* but changed his mind. He said I'd be what literary critics call "an unreliable narrator."

Me? Unreliable? I'd be objective while narrating the events, Tony's thoughts and his feelings. Well, at least I'd try to be honest, but, what the hell, I'm only human.

Anyway, I've got to get back into the pages—Oh, I almost forgot. What did Lou steal? Remember *Huckleberry Finn*? Or was it *Tom Sawyer*? I get the two mixed up. Mark Twain let a character from his former novel introduce the next one. It worked well for Twain, so Lou stole it. You can let him know if it worked in this book by purchasing it, or emailing him at loumacaluso@gmail.com.

Let's get started . . .

PROLOGUE

February 15, 6:10 p.m.

Her scream echoes between the pillars of the Victor Emmanuel Monument and resonates within Piazza Ara Coeli, then onto Piazza Venezia, down Via del Corso, and throughout Rome.

She had seen nothing.

It was that sound that triggers her shrieks and the impulse to cover her thirteen-year old daughter's eyes from the horror.

That sound.

She had first heard it over a decade ago, and she still recognizes it—not the crash of the first plane, or even the second that hit the Twin Towers. Those crashes shocked and stunned everyone into chaos. She sat trapped in her VW Bug on Trinity Place in front of the church, as hordes of people crushed through the streets, like bees swarming away from a fallen hive. She had dropped off her husband a few minutes earlier and pictured him setting his briefcase on his cubicle office desk on the eightieth floor of the World Trade Center.

That sound. A thud, not a dull thud. More like a quick loud splash, as if someone had dropped a heavy plastic bag filled with wet sand. She could barely turn her bloated pregnant body in the little bucket seat to see what had made that curious sound.

Her brain had trouble processing what her eyes had seen—a bundle of clothing meshed and glued together with a thick mixture of blood, flesh and bone. Her screams melded into the discord of shrieks and mayhem outside her car as she drove recklessly through the crowd.

But today her solo scream resounds away from the deserted historic monument and into the busy Roman streets. Even if it weren't near closing time, few tourists visit the Victor Emmanuel Monument during the winter off-season, on a cold misty day when the majestic Roman skyline hides in the fog from the monument's observation deck almost 300 feet above the pavement.

She descends the stairs and fights against the grain of people rushing to view the gruesome sight, which she visualizes far too well in her mind. She hails a cab as the squalling sirens of the *Polizia Municipale* and *Carabinieri* arrive. Soon the officers will fight through the crowd, discover the corpse, take charge and lie to the onlookers, "*non c'è niente da vedere* (there's nothing to see here)." They will search his pockets and identify the body as that of Todd Kenilworth.

PART I:

PALERMO, SICILY

CHESTER

July 10

"*Il signore che chi fara la conferenza*, Tony Morelli," said the head librarian at Biblioteca Centrale della Regione Siciliana, once a Jesuit college called Collegio Massimo dei Gesuiti, and now the home of Palermo's main public library.

Tony stepped to the podium and grinned like a kid about to deliver a book report to his grammar school class. The half-filled small auditorium produced a faint echo from the audience's applause.

This would be the last stop of a two-week book tour starting in Rome and ending in Palermo, sponsored by Pendler Press, the publisher of Tony's most recent book, *The Rise and Fall of Sal DeVanno, Italian-American*. Like his first non-fiction book *The Stagnant Clown*, a chronicle of James Dean's sense of humor, the Sal biography engendered only modest sales in the U.S., which didn't impress the Pendler execs; they were prepared to let Tony's two-book contract expire.

Due to the marketing finesse of Mick, Tony's agent and manager, Mick and Tony convinced the execs to test market a translated version of Sal in Italy. It seems that the story of an Italian-American Hollywood actor attaining and losing the American dream both captivated and fascinated Italian readers. Pendler not only extended Tony's contract for two more books, they sponsored this tour and paid for an interpreter to translate Tony's speeches.

"Since I am told that *ciao* can mean 'good-bye' in English, and *arrivederci* means 'I'll see you again,'" said Tony as he ended his speech and waited for the interpreter to translate for the audience, "I say from the bottom of my heart to you kind Palermo people, *arrivederci!*"

The crowd did not wait for the translation. They sensed Tony's warm farewell, cheered and awarded him a standing ovation.

Tony couldn't hold back a sigh of relief—his last stop on this Italian book tour. It was good that his speech was so well rehearsed, pauses for translation and all, because he couldn't concentrate on the words this time. He kept thinking about that guy sitting in the back row. He knew that face—or thought he knew it. Every time he'd look at the man for more than a few seconds the guy looked down as if trying to hide from Tony's stare.

It haunted Tony the whole time he sat at the table offstage and signed books for those who stood in line. Maybe the guy would buy a book, and he could ask him if they had met, Tony thought, but the mystery man didn't show.

"What's the matter?" asked Roberto, the Pendler interpreter who doubled as Tony's bookseller and travelling companion. "You seemed a little distracted today."

"It was a guy in the back row of the audience."

"The guy with the long, shaggy, gray hair in his fifties, about your age?"

"Yeah, you noticed him, too?"

"Only because every time you looked at him he seemed to look down and scratch the back of his head."

"I swear I've seen that guy before, or I know him or maybe knew him when we were both younger and better looking, but I can't place him. You ever experience that?"

"Sure, it's like, what's that French word for it?"

"Déjà vu?"

"That's it. It's something like that."

"I don't know. Maybe he just looks like someone from my past. My girlfriend, Pauline, is always accusing me of seeing people I think I know. One time I embarrassed the shit out of her in a restaurant. I was positive I knew this guy a few tables away. I walk up to his table and—"

Tony stopped as if he had felt a mild electric shock. "Pauline. I was supposed to call her after the speech. Excuse me, Roberto. I'm going to step outside these thick library walls where I can get better reception on my cell."

Roberto smiled and nodded. There was no reason for Tony to stick around. The auditorium had emptied, and Roberto would count the cash, pack the books and catch a cab back to the hotel on his own.

Tony stepped from the coolness of the old stone library and onto sunny Via Vittorio Emanuele. In mid-to-late July, the Sicilian sun always heated the windless Palermo streets. Unless you're in the city's center, much of Palermo looks tired and run-down because of the crumbling esoteric buildings, but it's a façade.

The people are vibrant, and the atmosphere is exciting, even a little dangerous. Laughter seeped through the beaded door curtain of a café/bar across the street. Tony thought he might step inside for a cold *limoncello* or a bottle of Moretti beer after he called Pauline.

Pauline had traveled with Tony for the first week of his tour but left after he spoke in Naples to start her own European tour. As a popular and respected jazz/blues singer throughout Chicago and the Midwest, she persuaded her manager to book a week of performances in France, where her recordings received some attention. Because the working portions of their trip overlapped for a week, they were able to celebrate together the anniversary of their eight-year relationship in Italy, where it had started.

They had met on a group tour of Italy where they tried running away from the emotional stress of failed marriages in the States.

Tony punched the first few numbers on his cell, and the strands of beads over the café/bar entrance jingled. A man stepped onto the sidewalk from the establishment. Tony glanced up from his phone. It was the guy with the familiar face in the audience. When the guy walked up the street, his identity hit Tony.

"Chet! I mean Chester! I mean Todd! Wait! It's Tony, Tony Morelli!"

Tony dodged the light traffic, crossed the street and trotted toward the man who ignored Tony's yells and broke into a run.

It was the guy's walk that jogged Tony's memory. He had grown up in the northwest Chicago suburb of Palatine, where Tony also grew up, until he was thirteen, when his family moved to the affluent south suburb of Flossmoor. His name was Todd Kenilworth, but everyone called him Chester from the then popular TV western series *Gunsmoke*. Chester was Marshall Matt Dillon's (James Arness's) deputy. Almost every episode seemed to feature Chester running down the Dodge City main street, exaggerating his characteristic stiff-legged limp and screaming "Marshall Dillon! Marshall Dillon!" whenever a crisis threatened Dodge.

A genetic defect in Todd's knee joint left him with a similar life-long staggered walk. It didn't hinder his athletic nature. He threw a mean fastball and became a legendary free-style swimmer within the south suburban high school conference.

Tony reached out and caught the guy's left shoulder; that's the last thing Tony remembered about his encounter.

Todd or Chester or whoever whirled and tagged Tony across the chin with a right hook that sent his body sideways before it slapped against the pavement.

O SOLE MIO

Tony's unconsciousness only lasted a few seconds, but it felt like hours to him. He awoke as a young couple pulled him to his feet, the girl asking over and over, "*Stai bene?* Tony assumed she asked if he was all right, and as a reflex answered, "I'm fine. I'm fine."

A small crowd had formed behind them.

The familiar voice of Roberto rang louder and louder as he broke through the people and said, "*Permesso. Permesso.*"

After the last polite crowd response of "*Prego,*" Roberto reached Tony and said, "What the fuck happened to you?"

"I got decked by Mr. Mysterious in the audience."

"What?"

"I'll explain on the way back to the hotel. Hail us a cab, and let's get out of here."

The small cluster of people dispersed, disappointed at the diminished excitement, and Roberto waved down one of the many taxis that roamed the Palermo side streets.

The driver hurried to help them load boxes of unsold books Roberto had piled on the sidewalk and escorted them into the car. Before asking their destination, he said, "Americans?"

"You got it," said Tony.

"Brand new taxi. Got satellite radio," he said like a kid anxious to show off a new toy. "What kind of music you want to hear?"

"How about some old Italian favorites?" Tony asked.

The driver shrugged, his disappointment obvious at Tony's choice, but he tapped the smart screen several times until Connie Francis's voice filled the cab with *O Sole Mio*.

"I love this song," said Tony.

"I love that female singer," said Roberto.

"Female singer. Pauline. Holy shit, I forgot to call her," he said almost as if he had taken another punch to the jaw. He retrieved his cell again from his pocket and called Pauline.

"What took you so long to call? Forget about me?" Pauline answered instead of the standard "Hello?"

"No, I was busy trying to break a guy's knuckles with my jaw."

"Huh?"

"I'm in a cab with Roberto on our way back to the hotel. Here's what happened," to Roberto, "Listen, so I don't have to tell this twice." He started with his recognition of the guy in the audience and finished with the couple standing him up.

"Are you okay?" Pauline asked with genuine concern.

"Yeah, sure. Just a little red mark. No swelling. My pride's going to be permanently scarred. I didn't think I could get sucker punched that easily."

"Sort of served you right, honey. Remember that time you thought Frankie Valli was sitting next to us at Petterino's Restaurant? You walked over to him and said, 'I really admire your work,' and the guy said in the deepest bass voice I ever heard, 'Did I ever do some plumbing work for you?' "

"Are you ever going to let me live that down?"

"Seriously," said Pauline, "how'd the speech go?"

"Pretty well, I think we sold about thirty books or so." He looked toward Roberto for confirmation, who nodded. "How's your tour going?"

"Excellent. Well, sort of excellent. The good news is actually sort of bad news."

"Let's hear it."

"Last night we finished at a beautiful old restaurant/winery in a vineyard, The Restaurant Kirmann in Epfig, with standing room only, but I almost didn't make it on stage. I accidently locked myself in my dressing room. When I got out it was like a maze in the building, I got lost and my cell phone wouldn't work."

"That's pretty funny, but not exactly bad news, unless the show didn't go well."

"Oh, no, the show was great, too great. I got more bookings right after we performed—some private parties and a place called Casa Loca in Haguenau. It means I have to extend the trip another week."

Tony's silence revealed his disappointment. They had planned to travel back to Chicago together. They would finish their anniversary celebration at their apartment in nearby Oak Park with a big party.

"Hey," he said after a long pause, "you can't get in the way of success. Go for it, girl."

"You're not mad?"

"No. Sure I'm a little disappointed, but what the hell. Like that guy in *The Producers* said, 'When you got it, flaunt it, baby.' I'll call Mick and have him cancel the party."

"Already done."

"You called him?"

"Yeah, and he has a surprise for you."

"Yeah? What?"

"You'll have to wait and see," she said, like a teasing little girl.

"Love ya."

"Love ya more, guy."

They ended the call just as the cab pulled up to their hotel, Palazzo Brunaccini. Tony loved old architecture, so this elegant historic building suited his tastes well. The young driver was probably happy to get these graying Americans and their "Old Italian Favorites" music out of his vehicle just as Jerry Vale broke into "Non Dimenticar" on the radio. A doorman offered to take the boxes of books up to Roberto's room, and Roberto accepted.

The two men stood outside and admired the ornate artistry in the arches and cornices, which characterized the windows and balconies of the hotel in the warmth of the setting Sicilian sun. A passerby might have taken them to be brothers. Although Roberto's bright blue eyes clashed with Tony's deeper set dark brown, both men towered around six-foot. Their wavy, salt-and-pepper curly hair and olive skin blended within the Italian culture they had shared for the past two weeks. Their personalities blended, also, and that often-discussed-but-not-clearly-defined male bond phenomenon developed early in their meeting.

"Well, partner, this is where we part company," Roberto said.

Tony looked at him as if Roberto had just confessed to murder, and remained speechless.

"Yeah, I know your flight leaves for Chicago tomorrow morning, but mine leaves for New York tonight. Guess Pendler Press would rather pay me to work in my office than to get drunk with you in the hotel bar."

"That's just what I had in mind for our last night in Italy," said Tony.

"Looks like you'll have to drink for both of us, Tony."

They exchanged a shoulder-to-shoulder buddy hug. Tony watched Roberto push through the revolving door and enter the lobby. He experienced a strange feeling, loneliness. Not that loneliness was strange to him. Before he had met Pauline, the months after his divorce, he had not only experienced loneliness, he rather enjoyed it; it gave him time to reflect on his life as a freelance writer, dependent on only Tony Morelli.

It sparked his creativity. He disciplined himself and began writing books—not just essays and short stories for meager paychecks from pop magazines, and the occasional literary journal. This loneliness felt strange because he had enjoyed the company of both Roberto and Pauline throughout the tour; it made the Italian experience richer because he was sharing it.

He put his hand up to his jaw and felt a lump. He hadn't lied to Pauline when he said it wasn't swollen. It either hadn't enlarged yet, or he hadn't noticed it.

Now that he was alone, he could feel pain. Why had that guy hit him? Even if it wasn't Todd, it seemed like an overreaction to a mistaken identity. *But it had to be Todd,* he thought, *that "Chester" limp.* Or was it just a freak coincidence? After all, he hadn't seen Todd in maybe forty years. It could have been someone whose likeness tweaked his memory in error.

The lobby's warm atmosphere dissipated his loneliness some. It was big and busy, but the dark red walls, overstuffed furniture and still-life paintings gave it a living room coziness. To the right and behind the reception desk, the hotel provided an office room complete with desks, computers and a printer for guests.

"What the hell," he said in a whisper to himself and sat down at one of the computers. He could have gone up to his room and used his own laptop (the hotel provided free Wi-Fi), but the empty room would amplify his loneliness. He Googled "Todd Kenilworth," but as expected, the search was too broad to yield a useful hit. After coupling the name with other key words including "Chicago," a news article surfaced. As Tony read it, his swollen jaw seemed to drop and nearly hit the keyboard.

SURPRISES

Tony picked up the copy of the article from the printer tray. He read it again as if the printed version might have details he had missed when he read it from the computer screen.

> American Attorney Leaps to Death
> Saturday, February 16
> (Translation courtesy of The Rome Sentinel)
> Rome police are investigating the apparent suicide of Todd Kenilworth, a 52 year-old attorney from Chicago, Illinois. Tourists discovered Kenilworth's body at the base of the Victor Emmanuel Monument around 17:40, just prior to closing time. The attorney apparently leaped from the nearly 80-meter high panoramic observation deck. No witnesses reported seeing the man jump. Pedestrians responded to a loud shriek.
>
> Police have not been able to locate the person who screamed or an elderly man seen leaving the staircase. Laura Kenilworth-DiFoggio (the deceased's sister) and her daughter, Rebecca, had accompanied Mr. Kenilworth on the trip to Rome.
>
> They reported that they were shopping in the city when the incident occurred. "Todd had been very despondent since his marriage broke up several years ago, our father's death around the same time and our recent decision to move my mother into a nursing home," said Ms. Kenilworth-DiFoggio. "This trip was supposed to cheer us all up. I guess it was all too much for my brother."

*****

He ate a Sicilian pizza (black olives and a baked egg in the middle) at a nearby outdoor café, had a few gin-and-tonics with lemon slices (rarely limes in Europe) at the hotel bar and retired to his room.

His room reflected the coziness of the lobby—dark red couch, hardwood floor and matching beamed ceiling. Tony had learned to accept the European style of small, quaint, simple room accommodations. After all, people didn't come to Europe to sit in their rooms. All day he was in denial that the trip had ended, but now reality hit him; his flight home was only hours away, so he began packing.

He took the folded article from his pocket and threw it in his suitcase. *Wait*, he thought, *I want to show this to Mick when he picks me up at the airport.* The article found a place in the outside pocket of his carryon bag.

He set his travel alarm for 4:30, and he let his body sink into the soft, thick feather mattress. His mind lingered in that transitional state between consciousness and sleep. He mumbled, "I saw Todd Kenilworth in Italy. But Todd died in Italy. Coincidence? Don't think so. Don't know."

*****

Mick hated picking people up at the airport. As a matter of fact, he and Tony hated airports. They never used to hate them. When they were kids, they would take the CTA (Chicago Transit Authority) bus to either O'Hare or Midway just to watch the planes and people come in. The excitement of travelers leaving for distant places or returning from long journeys vibrated throughout the terminal gate passageways, the little bookstores, coffee shops, boutiques and bars.

Sal DeVanno, the actor they knew from high school and subject of Tony's last book, would gather his actor/singer friends from West Chicago High, and they'd spend a Saturday or Sunday singing and doing skits at the terminals for tips. At O'Hare, where international flights land and take off, you could watch people go through customs and on occasion witness a drug bust.

Mick once said, "I'd rather scrape a tattoo off a fat politician's ass than visit an airport." Why? Tight security. He and Tony agreed that in this crazy world of terrorism, tyrant countries with nuclear bombs and nuts with automatic weapons, that extra precaution was necessary. But in their opinion, airport security had overreacted. Tony's words: "A numb-nuts tried to make a bomb from his shoelaces and only gets a hot-foot, and now we have to have to walk barefoot through security gates. Another attempted to detonate his boxers with his balls, and we must endure humiliating body scans.

Last month I left for New York and forgot to leave my thirty-nine cent K-Mart nail clippers in my luggage. They confiscated the clippers and delivered a thirty-nine cent security lecture. To avoid a strip search, I choked back my comment, 'Anyone who can highjack a Boeing 747 with my cheap nail clippers deserves the plane.'"

Tony looked terrible when he walked through the swinging doors with his luggage at O'Hare—hair mussed, swollen jaw, bags under his eyes, and wrinkled clothes.

"Don't you dare ask the obvious, cliché question," he said.

Naturally, Mick had to ask, "So, how was your flight?"

"Shitty, and fuck you for asking."

"You look like your seat was somewhere outside the plane."

"For nine hours I sat next to a four hundred pound Swedish guy. When his fat wasn't rolling into my lap, he honored me with his lengthy orations, laced with donkey-shit-smelling breath."

"Ah, how I missed your literary gift for poetic imagery."

Mick took his carryon bag, and Tony rolled his suitcase through the terminal. They didn't speak a word on their way to the outdoor parking lot. Guys who've known each other since kindergarten don't see the necessity of small talk. If Tony and Roberto could have passed as brothers, Tony and Mick couldn't even pass for the same species. Tony's tall, slender, Italian features gave him the look of an aging movie star in the autumn of his career. Mick's squat, stocky build, short, stiff haircut and Irish blue eyes made him look like his bodyguard as they strolled through the lot.

Mick stopped in the middle of Aisle B.

"Where's your car?" he asked as he twisted his disheveled body and scanned the lot.

Mick nodded at the brand new, bright metallic red Jeep Grand Cherokee in front of them—the sales sticker still attached to the passenger window.

"Wow! So you finally traded in that Columbo-car you've been driving for the past six years. Well, at least you had the good sense to buy the dream SUV I've been telling you about."

"It's not mine, partner. It's yours," Mick said and flipped the key fob to him.

Tony was so shocked he didn't even grab for it.

It hit the pavement, and the engine started.

NEW CAR, NEW CAPER

"What's going on?" asked Tony.

"It's a remote start," Mick answered.

"I know that, pin-head. I mean why the gift and from whom? Did my book make the Best Seller list? Did Pendler spring for an advance? Did you win the lottery and magically become less cheap and more generous?

"No, your book sales are up, but hardly in the best-seller class. Yes, I am one helluva guy, regardless of your disregard for my benevolent nature, but you're wrong on all counts. It's from Pauline—an anniversary gift and a product of her successful career."

"I don't deserve her."

"Yes, I agree, but let's load your stuff and get going. I hate airports."

Once over the shock, Tony acted like a little kid on Christmas morning. He could hardly wait to sit in the driver's seat and take Mick home. But his shocked expression returned when he buckled his seatbelt and saw the complex instrument panel.

"It looks like the cockpit of a fighter jet," he said.

Mick went over the buttons, knobs and switches just as the car dealer had done for him when he picked it up the day before. When Mick got to the Sirius satellite radio, Tony put his hand to his jaw. It reminded him of the experience just before his cab ride.

"By the way," Mick said, interrupting the tutoring session, "what happened to your jaw?"

"I got decked by Todd Kenilworth, or his ghost, or some guy that looked like Todd Kenilworth."

"What?"

Mick had known Todd from the neighborhood just as Tony had. As he backed out of the stall, Tony briefed him on his encounter with "Todd."

"So, you scared the shit out of this guy you thought was Todd, and he cold cocked you."

"It's not that simple, Mick—that 'Chester' walk? Reach back into the outer pocket of my carryon. There's an article I want you read."

Mick pulled out the article and read it twice.

"You might have something here, Tony. Too many coincidences: the limp, a Todd lookalike in Italy and Todd actually dying in Italy."

"That's what I thought."

They didn't speak during the whole trip from O'Hare to Mick's house in Naperville, a far west suburb of Chicago. He pulled into the driveway. They sat for almost a minute without speaking.

"You know what I'm going to say, don't you?" Mick broke the silence.

"Sure, 'Sounds like this could be your next book, Tony.'"

"Maybe. Maybe not. Look, Pendler isn't pressing you for another book yet, but they will be pretty soon. We've proven that your work has a small but respectable market here in the States, but a bigger, growing market in Italy. If you had a book set in both countries, it might expand both markets."

"What if I research it, and find out there's nothing to it or not enough for a book."

"Then all you wasted was a little time, and maybe there's enough for a feature essay, a short story or something I can peddle to a magazine here and abroad."

He felt his swollen jaw again and said, "I'll think about it."

"Don't think about it. Let me think about it. I'm the thinker. You're the writer."

He laughed and shook his head at the truth and irony of Mick's words.

"Hey, thanks for picking me up and obviously conspiring with Pauline on this surprise."

"Don't mention it. Like you said, you don't deserve her. Hey, we still on for our Friday ritual?"

"Count on it."

*****

Jennifer, Mick's "girlfriend-of-the-month" as Tony put it, and Mick had decorated his Oak Park apartment for a surprise anniversary party when Tony and Pauline came home. Since Pauline extended her tour, Mick cancelled the party but forgot to "un-decorate."

When Tony worked his key and opened the door, his first impression was the movie *The Lonely Guy*. In the film, Steve Martin and Charles Grodin, the lonely guys, throw a party but have no friends. Grodin decorates his apartment with crepe paper, party signs, streamers, and even life-size cutouts of celebrities.

"There's nothing drearier than a festive room without the festivities," he said to himself.

He deposited his luggage in his bedroom, went into the kitchen cupboard, found his bottle of DiSaronno, poured some into a snifter and sat at the table.

Todd Kenilworth, he thought. *Should I pursue this mystery or let it go and move on?* He reached for his loose change on the counter and pulled out a dime. He placed it on his fist over his thumb. With raised snifter he toasted, *"Déjà vu!"* (He had tried the same coin flipping technique when making the decision for his last book). For several seconds, he sat motionless like a bad imitation of a seated Statue of Liberty. He pictured himself and laughed out loud.

"Hell," he said, "it didn't work then; it won't work now. I know damn well what I'm going to do."

He gulped down his drink, opened his fist and let the dime drop into his palm.

KWL

Tony awoke, as usual, around ten o'clock. All night he had missed Pauline. He had gotten used to having her in his bed since she had moved in with him about a year earlier. Morning was different. Pauline, the earlier riser, always dressed and left the apartment by nine, even if she had sung until almost daylight at some club the night before.

Still in his robe and with a cup of fresh-brewed coffee in hand, he gazed out his second story patio window down onto Miller Street. He loved this late morning view of his neighborhood. The sun had risen well above Lake Michigan by now and illuminated downtown Chicago just a few miles east of his quieter but vibrant historic suburb, Oak Park.

Then, a new sight, his Jeep parked at the curb across the street, made Miller Street even more picturesque. The oak and maple trees along the parkway shading and protecting it, the thought struck how the vehicle reminded him of Pauline—the radiant red of her long wavy hair, her solid, but sleek and curvy body. He smiled and knew that like a kid with his favorite toy, Tony would gradually personalize his SUV and become attached to it like a little kid to a puppy.

He took his coffee to his office, adjacent to the living room. It was time to get to work. Tony's work routine always followed his decision to tackle a writing topic. The previous night he had made such a decision; he would pursue the mystery behind the life and death of Todd Kenilworth.

Tony sat at his solid oak desk and chair, which his beloved grandfather Sam Morelli had willed to him, the only other Morelli who encouraged him to pursue the unstable life of a writer instead of the more secure profession of businessman, doctor, lawyer or even teacher. The desk even had a hideaway drawer for that archaic writing tool, a typewriter.

He took out a blank sheet of paper and drew three columns. He labeled the first column K, the middle W and the third L. It was a teaching technique he had learned from his ex-wife, a high school English teacher. She used it for introducing a new unit.

For example, when teaching Macbeth, she would have the students list all the things they already knew about Shakespeare and/or Macbeth in the K (Known) column. They listed important questions about the play in the middle column (the What column) and, as they read the play and discussed the questions, important facts would go in the L (Learned) column. The KWL sheets also served as handy study guides for tests and essays. Tony adapted the strategy for his pre-research stage. It was about the only thing he had taken away from the divorce settlement.

Tony preconceived the development of his KWL sheet on Todd Kenilworth. The K column would be sparse with the few facts he knew about Todd when he lived in Palatine and information from the article about his death. He recalled that his father was a minister at the Methodist church and that his older sister, Laura, was a popular cheerleader at West Chicago High School. He didn't recall Todd's mother.

The Learned column would be blank but would build into pages and pages of facts as his research progressed. The What column was the most important. As Tony's ex told her classes, "Write good questions, and you'll get good answers," or in Tony's case, good facts to mold into a story.

Some questions emerged as natural as breezes off Lake Michigan into downtown Chicago: What happened to Todd after he moved from Palatine to Flossmoor? What about his law career? His marriage? His divorce? His family? What drove him to suicide? Why kill himself in Italy? Was there any connection with the guy who punched Tony and Todd?

More questions would evolve from the answers he gathered. This question-answer-question-answer cycle drove Tony's research and sometimes drove Tony near crazy whenever he tackled a writing project. After completing his preliminary list of questions, he sighed at the important question he needed to ask himself. *Where do I start?*

Hands behind his head, he sat back and rocked back and forth in his office chair. This room served as both an office and a sanctuary. His work desk, a computer work area, and Pauline's modern business bureau lined one wall. The two windows on that wall let in plenty of light and allowed Tony and Pauline to look over their desks at the Oak Park traffic on Harlem Avenue.

His high school geometry teacher had told Tony that you could learn a lot about a person just by looking at his or her desktop. Pauline's looked as if a serious, compassionate music teacher worked there. A few small plants requiring little attention, a picture of her and Tony at a wedding reception, another of her and her twenty-two year-old son dancing, several collectible figurines of singers and musicians, a matching desk set including a calendar/blotter and a name-plated gold pen and holder adorned her desktop.

Columbo's desk may have looked more organized than Tony's. The only cleared area was the five-year old calendar/blotter give-away from the Oak Park Community Library. It appeared as if Tony had put his arms in the middle of the blotter and through a pile of books, manuscripts, articles and loose papers, separated his arms and cleared the area for a place to work. He called his desktop his "artistic, creative clutter."

Pauline called it "a fucking mess."

He had a habit of putting himself into a trance. Years earlier he had taken a course called Stress Management to help him deal with the problems plaguing him during his ugly divorce. The course taught him a technique of self-hypnosis. When learning the technique, it takes a person about twenty minutes to put himself into a relaxed near-sleep state. With practice, one can do it in seconds. Tony found that self-hypnosis aided his writing. He could recall forgotten facts, solve plotting problems, and conjure new ideas.

In his dream-like state, he pictured himself batting in a Palatine Little League baseball game. Todd Kenilworth was the pitcher. There were no infielders, but the outfielders were

Todd's family as Tony remembered them. Todd's father wore his clergy collar and played left field. In deep center at the limit of visibility was Todd's mother. In her cheerleading uniform, his sister pounded her glove in shallow right field. Todd wound up and threw one of his famous flaming fastballs, but Tony saw the ball in slow motion and hit a high fly ball to . . .

He woke up and grabbed the desk phone receiver.

FAMILY TIES

"Didn't your aunt and uncle belong to the church in Flossmoor where Todd's father was the minister?"

"Don't you believe in standard greetings when calling someone on the phone?" Mick said.

"I know you have caller ID, smart ass. Now, save the lecture on proper phone etiquette and answer my question."

Mick had to think back. His Aunt Rita and Uncle Chuck lived in Homewood, the south suburb of Chicago adjacent to Flossmoor where the Kenilworths moved from the old neighborhood. "Come to think of it, they did go to his church, but all my aunts and uncles passed away years ago if you were looking toward them as a source. Sounds like you decided to investigate the Todd Kenilworth mystery?"

"Yeah."

That single word expressed dejection in Tony's voice.

"Don't sound so forlorn. Most churches have websites today, and I'm sure it has an archives or a history page. It had a long name like Peace United Church of Flossmoor or United Flossmoor Church of Christ or Flossmoor—"

Tony hung up.

He Googled several combinations of Mick's suggested church titles and discovered the website of Flossmoor United Church of Peace. As expected, the homepage conveyed a sunburst revelation and conservative symmetry. A low angle landscape shot of a modern looking red brick, tall steeple church building on a foreground of a spring green lawn, dotted with yellow and purple flower beds dominated central position of the page. A ghost-like, superimposed Christ figure with opened arms and a backlight of sunrays hovered in the blue sky. The scripture, ". . . seek and you will find. . . " Matthew 7:7, in italic black lettering stenciled on the green grass.

A Coming Events column bordered the photo on the right. The web menu fringed the left side. Tony scrolled down the headings and clicked on the title, CHURCH HISTORY. The first few paragraphs recorded a brief saga of this Protestant denomination that dated back to the early 1900s. The next several pages detailed this Flossmoor church's history from its onset in 1952. Whenever the church installed a new pastor, a family picture of that minister appeared next to the text.

He scanned the article until he recognized the Kenilworth family photo dated 1967. The photograph featured a tall, rugged, athletic-looking minister standing behind a prim, smiling woman seated in a cushioned cane-back chair. Reverend Kenilworth stood as if he were supported by a rigid stand behind him. He wore a long-sleeved white tab-collared dress shirt and a thin black silk tie with a sparkling diamond tie-tack pinned halfway down it.

The woman's modest smile suggested she was responding to the photographer's command. Her short wavy blond hair seemed longing to grow out and accentuate her green eyes, sculptured face, and curvy body in a tight-fitting, long grass green dress that barely covered white high heels at the bottom and cleavage at the top. Her hands were folded neatly in her lap.

Two children sat as happy, obedient offspring at her feet. Todd smiled like he had just hit a Little League homerun and displayed a missing front tooth. He wore a plaid starched short-sleeved sport shirt, dark pants and Buster Brown dress shoes. His crossed legs exposed a hint of white athletic socks that clashed with his outfit.

His older sister sat with her legs tucked sideways beneath a plaid skirt. She wore a fluffy white sweater upstaging her long, ironed dirty-blond hair inherited from her mother. Her insincere smile might have been the product of prodding and coaching from her parents and the photographer before the camera flashed. Todd stood out for some reason. Tony couldn't pinpoint it, but he appeared out of place from the others.

The text only revealed that Reverend David Kenilworth had led the church as head pastor from 1967 until his retirement in 1990.

Tony went back to the website menu and clicked on the Archives title. This section listed all the bimonthly church newsletters from 1964 to the present. He decided to download all the issues from 1967 and search for information about the Kenilworths. The 1967 May/June publication included the same family picture as in the history section. The copy revealed that "Reverend David Kenilworth entered the U.S. Army in 1946 and served in Italy during post-war military operations. When he returned to the States in 1950, he married his longtime sweetheart, Beth Carver."

Subsequent issues chronicled typical church events: weddings, funerals, fund-raisers, potluck suppers, confirmation classes, Sunday school pictures and so on.

One headline from a fall 1979 copy snagged Tony's attention: PASTOR K PRESIDES AT DAUGHTER'S WEDDING.

Pastor Kenilworth had the honor of serving as both father-of-the-bride and deliverer-of-the-vows when daughter, Laura, and Terrance DiFoggio wed on Saturday, October 7.

A blurry, black-and-white photo of the newlyweds posing on the altar steps accompanied the brief, amateurish article. The name, Terry DiFoggio, rang a faint bell in Tony's head but not loud enough to interrupt his current research of the Kenilworths.

Tony skimmed the humdrum articles within the next decade of newsletters. Nothing piqued his interest until a 1990 issue announced "the retirement of Pastor Kenilworth." The forgettable article didn't offer any pertinent information, but the photo page did.

It presented a collage of church pictures featuring the family and featured a "Then and Now" photo comparison. The photographer posed the family in the same manner as they appeared in the 1967 photo when the pastor and family joined the congregation and presented the pictures side-by-side. Of course, they had aged in a predictable manner, but the prints looked eerily similar. Laura exhibited the same phony smile, and Todd still emerged as the misfit of the family.

This appeared to be the end of the church newsletter archive's value as a resource. Just for the hell of it, Tony decided to skim the rest of the publications for more information, and it paid off. An issue only three-years old, reported, FORMER PASTOR KENILWORTH DIES OF NATURAL CAUSES. The story revealed that he had died at peace in his home, and it listed the funeral arrangements. The rest was a sloppy compilation of cutting-and-pasting from former newsletter articles to summarize his affiliation with the church. Two years later, an article featured his wife in the NEWS FROM PEACE VALLEY column. The church had founded and funded a retirement community, Peace Valley, just a communion wafer's throw from the church building. The column consisted of one-sentence information snippets. A clip dated from just the previous year reported:

Peace Valley welcomes Beth Kenilworth, wife of former Pastor David Kenilworth.

Tony shut down his computer and reached for the key fob of his new Jeep.

PEACE VALLEY

The engine purred like a healthy sleeping lion as Tony contemplated the best route from his Oak Park apartment to Flossmoor, Illinois, thirty miles straight south. A GPS search predicted the I-294 toll road as the quickest path. Tony knew that major road construction, started in the summer and projected to end by Christmas, proved the GPS to be a false prophet. The next suggestion was the Eisenhower Expressway toward downtown Chicago and the Dan Ryan Expressway south to Flossmoor. The odds of the Dan Ryan not being backed up due to an accident were about as good as Mick giving up women and choosing the priesthood.

Tony settled on Harlem Avenue, a half block from his home, straight south to Flossmoor Road. It was the most direct course, but the most tedious and least efficient due to the many stoplights and heavy traffic; however, it gave him time to think.

"How can Mrs. Kenilworth help me? What questions can I ask that won't disturb her, open wounds about the past? Will she even talk to me? What state of mind is she in?" Tony asked himself as he turned onto Harlem.

People who watched Tony drive alone might have thought he was talking on a speaker phone, singing to music or displaying psychotic behavior. He talked to himself when he felt completely alone. It was his way of organizing his thoughts. It was as if his thoughts materialized and allowed him to visualize and to synthesize them in a meaningful way.

The long stretch of stop-and-go traffic kept Tony quizzing himself, and the more he quizzed himself, the more he doubted the potential for this Todd Kenilworth project. "Todd is dead. He killed himself. Questioning his mother about it will only upset her. So, why am I doing this? It's that unique limp, the resemblance and his reaction," Tony said and felt his jaw. The swelling had already diminished to a slight bulge.

By the time he reached the three-miles of wooded area of the far south Chicago suburbs, he had exhausted himself with his introspective quiz show routine. The peacefulness turned his thoughts toward Pauline. *Wonder what she's doing now. Where is she? Who is she with? Does she still love me? Of course she does, dumb ass. She bought you this car, didn't she? Wait until she sees what I got her. I wonder—shit!*

A deer.

The mammoth sized horned creature appeared as if by magic in front of his Jeep. He locked his brakes, swerved right and prepared for the crash. His outside rearview mirror must have shaved the outer bristles of the deer's white tail. His SUV dipped into and out of the ditch like a rollercoaster and came to a stop, perpendicular to Harlem at the gravel shoulder. His heart beat like a Gene Krupa drum roll, as he looked back at the road.

The deer stared at him as if to say, "So, what's your problem?" and sauntered across Harlem and into the thick woods.

"I hope you're not an omen," said Tony.

He turned off Harlem onto, of all streets, Oak Park Avenue. How ironic, he thought, the only road that leads to Flossmoor Road possesses the name of my neighborhood, thirty miles north of here. Old well-kept mansions bordered Flossmoor Road for a few miles in a populated residential community, until more modern homes spread out into a wooded area.

Just beyond a steep stretch of road, Flossmoor United Church of Peace loomed into view, the same as it appeared on the website. Tony almost imagined the ghost-like Christ in the background. An arrow sign indicated that Peace Drive, behind the church, led to Peace Valley Retirement Community.

"Shit," said Tony when he saw that the gated private village had a security guard house.

A skinny, uniformed clean-cut young man sat watching a TV screen at the opened window when Tony drove up to the gate.

"I'm here to see Beth Kenilworth," Tony offered.

"Do you know where you're going?" asked the young man whose attention never left the TV screen.

"Not exactly."

"Then sign in at the reception desk in the community center. Just follow the circular drive."

Not exactly Fort Knox, Tony thought as he drove toward the wooded curving pavement. He felt as if he were entering a wealthy vacation resort. The roadway circled a natural-looking pond with geese and ducks swimming in small groups to the left. Only four spots marked VISITORS allowed for parking, and those were filled. He drove by the entrance of the main building and parked in one of the numbered parking spaces marked RESERVED.

What the hell, Tony thought, *these are elderly people, and I'm sure most don't drive anymore.* He pulled into space 115 and walked toward the automatic sliding doors. A couple holding hands and operating their electronic wheelchairs nearly ran over Tony.

"Think fast, partner," said the elder gentleman, "Peace Valley can be Death Valley when you're not alert."

They all laughed, and Tony stepped inside. He couldn't stop himself from saying aloud, "Wow! I feel like I'm in that old movie, *Grand Hotel*."

A merry-go-round sized chandelier hung low over an indoor pond trimmed with tall, leafy indoor plants. High backed living room furniture on warm colored circular rugs formed several conversation areas surrounding the pond. Opposite the entrance, a glass wall separated the lobby from an outdoor patio where people could sit on cushioned iron chairs and view a small lake with a fountain in the center where geese and swans bathed.

"Can I help you, sir?" asked a middle-aged woman seated behind the hotel-like reception counter to the right.

"Yes, I'd like to visit Mrs. Beth Kenilworth."

"Are you a relation?"

If I tell the truth, Tony thought, *they may have stupid rules, and I won't be allowed to see her. If I lie, they might be able to check with ease and I could be escorted out.*

"Well, sort of a relative. Her son, Todd, and I were very close as children, and she was like a second mother to me."

A half-truth seemed appropriate.

Tony scanned the lobby. It almost looked like a silent movie. Every conversation area contained from two to five residents—white-haired women and some men with bad toupees, all talking but nary a sound resonated to the front desk.

The receptionist hung up a phone and said, "She said she would meet you in the library room. It's just to the left." She pointed past the chandelier.

"Thank you."

As he passed through the lounge, the conversation level raised to only a low murmur. He seemed to be invisible to them unless he walked close to someone, and then the person would say, "Hello" as if he had materialized out of nowhere.

The library reminded Tony of the hotel lobby in Palermo: warm, homey furniture and paintings. The bookshelves lined the walls but only extended as high as a wheelchair reader could reach. Only one silver-haired woman in a wheelchair sat reading from a stack of poetry books on a lamp table in the corner.

Tony chose one of two high-back cushy chairs with a coffee table between them and sat. He marveled at the quietness and serenity, despite the openness and activity of the Community Center. People using canes, walkers and wheelchairs passed the garden/chandelier center as Tony absorbed the tranquil atmosphere.

A tall, bent over woman, obstructed his view as she stood at the library entrance. She perused the room and skimmed past Tony as if he were invisible.

He recognized her from the family picture on the church website. Yes, age had thinned and grayed her hair, but she wore it in the same short, wavy style. Her dress, similar in fashion to the one she wore in the photo, hung rather than clung to her slender body.

"Excuse me, ma'am," he said. "I'm Tony, Tony Morelli. I'm the man who came to see you."

She squinted at him and then focused. Her expression went from bewilderment to curiosity to disappointment.

"But you're not my son. You're not Todd. I thought she said Todd came to see me."

"No, Mrs. Kenilworth, that's what I came to talk to you about," Tony said and led her by her arm to a chair.

THE CONVERSATION

"I'm sorry about the misunderstanding, Mrs. Kenilworth," said Tony. He felt sympathy and compassion for the woman. His first goal would be to erase the tense, confused look on her face. Next, he would try to elicit the truth about her son without opening old emotional wounds. "You see, I knew Todd when we were kids from our old neighborhood, before you moved to Flossmoor. My name is Tony Morelli. We played Little League baseball on different teams. I faced his famous fiery fastball many times."

Mrs. Kenilworth's eyes drifted up toward the ceiling, and she maintained her taut expression as if she were trying to recall something. Her facial muscles relaxed into an introspective smile, and her grayish eyes met Tony's. "I'm sorry, Mr. Morelli, I honestly don't remember you, but then, I didn't know many of Todd's friends. Being a minister's wife was a busy job back then. I do remember him playing baseball. How he loved baseball."

Tony reflected a grin back to her and nodded. He had achieved his first goal. Now, he must find out about Todd. Tony had majored in journalism and minored in broadcasting in college. Before evolving into a freelance writer, his objective was to be Walter Cronkite. Journalistic training had taught him that there were two distinct methods of drawing information from an interviewee—either act as if you know more than you do and let the subject fill in the blanks, or act as if you know very little. Tony opted for the "act stupid" approach.

"Actually, I wanted to contact Todd. As a writer, I'm always interested in people from my past. Sometimes reconnecting with them leads to interesting stories that I can use in articles, essays and sometime books. Do you know how I might get in touch with him?"

That anxious look returned to her face. Tony felt bad. Maybe he had gone too far and opened that emotional wound.

"I'm sorry, Mr.?"

"Morelli."

"Mr. Morelli, Todd is no longer with us."

"Really? I am so sorry."

"Yes, he, his sister and my granddaughter went on a trip to Italy last winter and—"

"That's okay, Mrs. Kenilworth, you don't have to—"

"And Todd decided to live there."

Now it was Tony's turn to tighten his facial muscles. *What did this mean? Was that really Todd in Palermo? Is he still alive? How could he be alive if he killed himself in Rome? Is the family keeping Todd's suicide a secret from his mother? Is her aged mind protecting her and keeping it a secret from herself? Keep her talking,* Tony told himself.

"That's interesting," said Tony, "because I thought I saw him when I was in Italy a few days ago."

"You did? How is he?"

Tony felt his still tender jaw. "Well, if it was him, it's hard to say. He was kind of in a hurry. What made him decide to stay there?"

"I'm not sure. All my information came from Laura, my daughter." Her focus went to the carpet when she mentioned her daughter's name. "My daughter and I don't speak much, but Todd has a right to live where he wants. He had a successful career as a lawyer and a rather painful divorce."

"When did you last speak with Todd, Mrs. Kenilworth?"

She looked down at a lacey hanky she had been fidgeting with during the conversation, and a tear formed in the corner of her eye. "He called in May and wished me a happy birthday."

I have gone too far, Tony thought. Either Todd is alive, or the family is going to great lengths to keep his death a secret from his mother. Either way, he couldn't verify the truth here, and he could only cause more pain to this woman.

"I'm sorry, Mrs. Kenilworth. I'll leave you now. Before I go, is there any way I can contact your daughter, Laura?"

Beth Kenilworth sat up straight. Her fidgeting turned to fists that clenched her handkerchief. "My daughter and I are not very close, never were. Then, she married that . . ." She stopped herself. She either felt she had gotten herself too worked up, divulged too much family information or maybe both. "I'm sorry, Mr. Morelli. Laura lives near here in Tinley Park, one of those new subdivisions, Garden Park or Garden Lane, or something like that."

"Thank you, Mrs. Kenilworth," Tony said and stood, "for your time and generosity with information."

She held out her hand, and he shook it with both his hands. As he left the library, he turned from the lobby and said, "And if I should see Todd, I'll tell him his mother is doing well at Peace Valley."

She stood up, faced him and yelled as if she were scolding a child, "Todd's mother is not some decrepit old woman in a nursing home!"

The outburst caused everyone in the lobby to look at him.

Tony didn't know how to react. He headed toward the exit. A thin, gaunt geriatric gentleman supported himself with a cane at the door. He appeared to be shaking.

"Everything's going to be okay, sir," Tony said, patted him on the shoulder and left, only to be shocked again when he stepped outside.

SISTER ACT

The skinny security guard stood behind Tony's Jeep listening to a blond woman waving her gold jewelry clad arms and ranting. She had left her glimmering Lexus running with the driver's door opened and parked across the road.

As Tony approached, the two looked at him. The guard, who had paid no attention to him when he drove in, squinted as if he needed to catch every detail of Tony for a police report. The woman's glare matched the guard's with an added venomous grimace. The blond wig sat like a cat half on and half off a volleyball, and saucer-size tortoise rim sunglasses almost masked her over-tanned, leathery, thin, prune face. Even her skimpy leopard spotted dress hung on her emaciated body and revealed knobby varicose legs teetering on stiletto pumps.

"She looks like a hockey stick with hair on it," Tony murmured to himself.

"Is this your car?" asked the guard in a feeble effort to sound authoritative and tough. "This is this lady's parking spot, and she is very upset."

Tony smiled and scanned the many empty numbered spots. "No," he said and put on his best Joe Pesci madman face to join the angry atmosphere, "but I know the son-of-a-bitch who owns it, and I'll move it."

He hopped into his Jeep and drove away.

*****

The downside to being Tony's literary agent/business manager and his best friend is that Tony often forgets that he's not Mick's only client. In the middle of signing a well-known best-selling writer who left his longtime New York agent, Mick's cell phone rang.

"Mick, stop what you're doing."

"No."

"Yes, this is important."

"So is signing John Grisham as a client."

"You're signing John Grisham to a contract!"

"Not exactly John Grisham, but almost."

"Well, then, listen, I just want you to do something for me. It'll just take a minute."

"Where are you?"

"I'm at Fox's Pub, a bar/restaurant in Orland Park not far from the retirement community where I just talked with Todd's mother."

"Two questions: Did you find out anything important, and have you had too many Augustiners (Tony's favorite German Hefeweissbier)?"

"No, I've had just one Hacker-Pschorr; they don't have Augustiner, and second, yes, either the family is keeping Todd's suicide a secret, Mrs. Kenilworth is senile, or Todd is still alive and that was him who clipped me in Italy. The only one who knows which story is true is Todd's sister, Laura.

"According to the mother, she lives close by, in Tinley Park. Thought I'd pay her a visit while I'm here on the south side. I don't have my computer with me, and can't get good internet reception on my smart phone. You know that people-finder website we subscribe to, the one I use to look up leads on people I'm writing about, and you use to look up potential clients and girlfriends?"

"Yeah."

"Look up Laura, I think her married name was DiFoggio, and see if you can get her address, phone, whatever and call me back on my cell."

"Just put 'John Grisham' on hold and do this?"

"Sure, it'll just take a minute."

Both men knew their friendship trumped about everything except Tony's relationship with Pauline, and sometimes she questioned Tony's loyalties.

Mick called him back after a few minutes of checking.

"Are you sitting on a sturdy barstool with a tall Hacker-Pschorr handy?" Mick asked.

"You betchya."

"Laura Kenilworth-DiFoggio lives at 8816 West 195th Street, Gracious Manor, in Tinley Park. Sounds like one of those subdivisions near I-80. No phone listed. She must just use a cell."

"None of that sounds earth shaking."

"I'm not done. She's a widow. Her ex was Terry DiFoggio. Brother of the late, notorious Richard DiFoggio... Tony, are you still there?"

Tony must have choked a little on his beer. Everyone in the Chicago area knew the story about Richard DiFoggio. He ran DiFoggio Construction, a legitimate business that also fronted for mob operations. Despite the scandalous connection, the company enjoyed a reputation as a topnotch railroad construction firm.

In the 80s, Mayor Jane Byrne contracted DiFoggio Construction to extend the Blue Line Subway System to include O'Hare Airport, linking tourism and business travel with downtown hotels, restaurants and other lucrative, taxed businesses. Somehow Richard got caught skimming company profits and paying off mob figures. A few weeks before he was scheduled to testify before a grand jury involving tax fraud, workers found his dead body at the Blue Line construction site with three bullets to his head.

Tony recovered from his shock and said, "I didn't even know there was another DiFoggio son."

"Evidently Terry, Dick's brother, was the 'Fredo of the family?"

"What?"

"You know 'Fredo from The Godfather, the weak brother. Only Terry was even more of a 'Fredo than The Godfather 'Fredo. Laura's husband seemed to have no connection with the family business. He was an insurance agent in New York."

"Really?"

"There's more. He worked at one of the Twin Towers during 9/11. It was reported that he was one of the people who jumped to his death. Sound familiar?"

*****

It was 4:45 p.m. Tony only had three unbreakable rules in his life: never let a Dave Clark Five song play too long on the radio, avoid rush hour traffic at all times and don't drink more than a couple beers before five o'clock. As he turned off "I'm in Pieces" from the 60s satellite radio station and lumbered his new Grand Cherokee along the bumper-to-bumper traffic south on Harlem Avenue toward Tinley Park, he realized that he had broken all three rules that day.

A concrete plaque on a brick wall read, "Entering Gracious Manor" on 195th Street. Tony turned into the subdivision, a typical far south Chicago suburban housing development—different models of the same two-car garage house and no trees.

The house at 8816 West 195th sat just three blocks from busy Harlem Avenue at the start of a circular drive that dead ended the street. Two girls wearing baseball gloves and uniforms played catch in the circular drive. Tony parked his Jeep about a half block away. *No sense risking a dent in my new ride.* Laura's house appeared to be one of the more modest models—no second story over the attached double garage. As Tony cut across the driveway toward the front door one of the girls playing catch said, "Can I help you?"

"You live here?" Tony asked.

"Who wants to know?" she returned.

It sounded more like a disrespectful challenge than a question. Thirteen or fourteen. Junior high school. Just that obnoxious age when they think they know more than anyone twice their age and older. But Tony didn't take offense. After all, he was a stranger, and there was the probability she had been lectured about being cautious.

"My name's Tony Morelli. I was a boyhood friend of Todd Kenilworth. I was told Laura, his sister, lived here. I was in the neighborhood and recently heard about his passing. Just thought I'd stop by and offer my condolences."

The girl put her head down as if to hide her emotions, approached him and said, "That was my uncle." She took off her cap, and a thick crop of blond, wavy hair flopped to her shoulders. "Follow me, but wait here on the porch. Mom just got home from work and might be in the shower."

Before she disappeared behind the white, metal screen door, he read the name DIFOGGIO embroidered over her number. She also had a slight limp, similar to her uncle's.

He scanned the neighborhood from his front door vantage point. The other girl amused herself by throwing high pop ups with the softball and misjudging them as they hit the concrete.

Something seemed wrong. It was a pleasant July late afternoon, not hot, clear sky, but quiet. Almost too quiet, even with busy Harlem Avenue only a few blocks away. *Sterile, that's the word, No personality, not like the old neighborhoods. Open. Only a few young trees providing neither shade nor shadows. Except for these two softball players, everyone else must be locked inside watching screens: TVs, computers, Kindles, smart phones.*

"Can I help you?" Laura Kenilworth-DiFoggio said from the inside.

The indoor darkness and tight mesh screen made it impossible for Tony to make out her features, just a slight figure wrapped in a thick, white bathrobe and a matching towel swathed around her head.

"Remember, you said you'd drive me to the ballpark in a half hour," the girl said, opened and slammed the door behind her as if she were afraid to let the sunlight indoors.

"You still haven't told me how you're getting home, Rebecca," said Laura.

"I'll walk," she answered without turning and rejoined her friend on the street.

"Not if it's too dark and not with a bunch of boys following, miss!"

Tony waited for more discussion, but muteness indicated that this routine dialogue had ended. He broke the silence, "I'll bet she's a pitcher."

"Sorry?"

"I said, I bet she's a pitcher with a wicked fastball like her uncle Todd."

"Oh, right. Becky said you knew my brother. Come on in and make yourself at home in the living room while I go upstairs and put something on."

Tony had to let himself inside and only caught a glimpse of her bare feet at the top of the stairs. He stood beneath the archway to the living room and said just above his breath, "Just as sterile as the outside."

Plain white walls, beige carpet, dull brown furniture, modern glass coffee table and a big screen TV. Only one picture was centered on the unadorned mantel over the fireplace. Tony walked toward it for a closer look. It was the same family photo he had seen online with the article announcing Reverend Kenilworth as the new pastor.

"I'm afraid our family dynamics have changed drastically since that Father Knows Best picture was taken."

Gorgeous. Tony almost uttered this single thought. In her tight cutoff shorts and sleeveless Chicago Cubs t-shirt, she looked the same to him as his memory of her in her Palatine High School cheerleading uniform.

"Laura DiFoggio," she said, walked towards him and extended her hand.

"Tony Morelli. I apologize for barging in like this, but I was in the neighborhood on business. A friend of mine and I were reminiscing about our childhood recently, and Todd's name came up. I learned about his unfortunate accident and that you lived in the area. I just thought I'd drop by and offer my condolences."

"Well, it was hardly an accident, but thank you." She lowered her head, similar to the way her daughter and mother had done earlier. Her long damp blond hair lay flat on her shoulders. When she lifted her chin, age wrinkles lined the tan, leathery skin on her neck. Somehow, she still looked young and attractive. "I'm sorry, Tony, but I don't remember you. When did you say you knew Todd?"

"It was before you moved to Flossmoor, when Todd was in Little League."

She threw her head back and laughed. "That's why I don't remember. I was around her age," she nodded toward the window where her daughter could be seen playing catch outside, "or maybe older. I focused on more important things like boys, cheerleading, appearances and boys, although she seems as interested in baseball as boys."

Tony just smiled and wondered how he could direct the conversation back toward Todd.

"Which reminds me," she continued, "I guess I don't have much time to chat, but can I offer you a beer or something?"

Tony noted that it was after five, but decided not to bend his third rule any further.

"No, thank you. Listen, if it's too painful for you to discuss, I understand, but I was so shocked when I heard how Todd died. What happened, Laura?"

She took a deep breath and closed her eyes.

Her next words, Tony thought, might be "I'm sorry, I don't want to talk about it."

Her eyes opened. She stared straight at Tony and said, "Okay, you seem like a genuine friend of Todd's, so I'll do my best and try to explain."

Her stare redirected outside the window, but she seemed to be looking beyond the girls. "I guess it all started with his divorce a few years ago. Yeah, that's when we started to see a change in Todd. He really loved Lou Anne, and I guess she loved him, at least in the beginning. But after he got his law degree and landed some rich clients and contracts, Lou Anne started loving the money more than him. When Todd called her on her heavy spending, she'd berate him and call him 'cheap.' She may have thought divorcing him and getting a big settlement and alimony was easier than trying to squeeze dollars out of him while they were married."

She focused back on Tony and said, "Big mistake. Never mess with a smart attorney."

Tony stared back at her. His journalism background kicked in. Interviewing Rule: When a subject feels comfortable talking, let him/her talk. The story will come out, even if the person doesn't want to tell it. He maintained an interested and innocent expression.

Laura squinted toward the window and continued, "Anyway, it was an ugly divorce. Todd was really broken up. Shortly before that, Dad had died, and then we had to put my mother in a nursing home. Todd was very close to my parents. I thought our trip to Italy would do him some good, maybe snap him out of his depression. I was wrong. I guess his suicide is partly my fault."

Normally, this would be Tony's cue to offer some consoling words, "No one can protect someone from himself," etc. But there was no guilt present in her tone. She just continued staring through the window.

After a minute of awkward silence, Tony said, "I think it's a kind thing you've done for your mother—keeping Todd's death a secret from her."

"What!"

"I visited your mother at the retirement home. She talked about speaking with your brother."

"Who do you think you are, visiting her? You're not family. She's a confused old woman. You've no right. Who are you really, Mr. Morelli? Why this sudden interest in my brother?"

Time to come clean, thought Tony. "I'm a writer, Laura, and a former friend of Todd's. I thought his life and death might make an intriguing story. Actually, what stirred my curiosity was that I thought I had encountered him or someone that looked like him while I was doing a book tour in Italy."

"Get out. Get out now, or I'll have you arrested."

"I'm sorry. I didn't mean to—"

"Now."

Tony let himself out and walked to his car.

"Well, that went well," he said and started the engine.

Rebecca threw a high pop up to her friend. This time she caught it.

FRIDAY NIGHT RITUAL

"'Get out!' Those were her words, Mick, so I left with my tail between my legs."

Tony had just relayed the scene from the day before at Laura Kenilworth-DiFoggio's house. Mick and Tony were enjoying the all-you-can-eat antipasto buffet at Trattoria #10's downstairs restaurant/bar in downtown Chicago. This had become their five o'clock Friday night ritual whenever they were both in town. Tony's usual routine was to excuse himself at about eight o'clock, so he could catch Pauline's singing gig at one of the Chicago blues clubs. Pauline wouldn't be back from her European tour until Monday, so they had all night to talk about this Todd Kenilworth book idea.

"So, what do think, Mick? Did I blow it? Am I the insensitive asshole in this one?

"Yes, you're an asshole; we both know that. Insensitive? Back up to when she snapped. What did you say just before that?"

Tony peered through the foam atop his tall glass of Augustiner Hefeweissbier as if his words were somewhere in the rich, hoppy wheat beer.

"I mentioned that I had visited her mother and complimented her on keeping Todd's suicide a secret . . . No, wait. Just after that, I told her that I thought I saw Todd in Italy."

"It might be that you are an insensitive prick, I mean asshole, and she just overreacted to your meddling in her family affairs. But I've got a hunch it's more than that. Seeing Todd or his double or his ghost coupled with knowing about the mother and the suicide cover-up seemed to hit a nerve. Maybe there's a connection there and maybe not. If there is, there's probably a helluva story behind it all, which means another book idea. The only way to find out is to keep snooping."

"Great, but where do I go from here? Apparently I've burned the bridges between me and all the living relatives."

It was nearing seven p.m., the end of the antipasto buffet. Between the after work crowd and the dinner mob, the basement bar became quiet and empty. The darkness may have seemed romantic for couples, but for Tony and Mick the emptiness only intensified their lack of an answer to Tony's question.

"So, when's Pauline due back?" Mick asked the rhetorical question. It broke the tension. Also, Mick knew Tony's subconscious seemed to work better than his conscious mind. Thinking about something else sometimes triggered his subliminal thoughts toward an answer.

"Monday."

"What did you get her?"

Tony choked a little as he sipped his beer.

"That's another mystery I haven't solved. How do I top or even equate a brand new car? Pauline's tough enough to buy for. She's not materialistic, but sentimental. Now my ex—"

Tony looked as if someone had hit him with a stun gun.

"That's it," he said.

"What?"

"Pay the tab. I'll hail a taxi," he said, gulped down the rest of his beer and ran up the stairs.

COME ON INN

Lou Anne Kenilworth.

Todd and Mick must have Googled Todd's widow's name with every possible key word combination in the English language.

"I feel like I'm in one of those teen computer movies from the 80s. You know, where a young Matthew Broderick or Christian Slater spends half the movie staring, wide eyed into a computer screen," said Tony.

"Yeah, except in those movies the hackers always broke into a corporation's or the government's computer system. We can't even locate a person," Mick said, lit a cigarette and walked toward his office window. Mick's second story office overlooked renowned Rush Street in downtown Chicago.

Rush Street was known for its nightlife—bars, restaurants, party atmosphere, especially on weekends. When Harry Caray announced Cub games, Chicago christened him with the unofficial name, the Mayor of Rush Street, because of his legendary presence there during Cub home stands.

Mick's office could have been termed a mini man cave—wood paneled walls, black leather couch, matching desk chair, and a few darkly varnished chairs facing his desk. Unlike Tony's Columbo-style untidiness, he prided himself on orderliness.

Tony leaned back in the desk chair, pushed himself away from the computer and stared at the white ceiling tiles. Below, Rush Street rocked in its characteristic party mode, geared up for a warm summer weekend night. Singles bar-hopped in small and large groups. The promise of finding a soul mate or a one-night stand swelled with every flashing colored light. About a dozen beer saturated young women singing off key burst out of Pippen's Tavern down the street. One of them wore a white wedding veil that just clung to the side of her head.

"Hey, didn't you say that there was an article about Laura's wedding in that newsletter on that church website?" Mick asked.

"Yeah."

"Wasn't there one about Todd's wedding?"

"That's funny. I don't remember seeing one. Of course I just skimmed and scanned those boring archived church bulletins. Let me check again."

Now the pair looked like two astonished Matthew Brodericks (only much older) from an 80s teen-computer-hacker movie as they read the tiny announcement from the church newsletter:

Mario and Angelina Rossi of South Bend, Indiana announce the engagement of their daughter, Lou Anne, to Todd Kenilworth, son of Reverend David and Beth Kenilworth of Flossmoor. The couple plans to marry in June at Saint Joseph Catholic Church, South Bend...

"Wonder why they didn't follow up and have a big deal article about the wedding like they did for Laura's wedding," said Tony.

"I can see two possible reasons just in that little announcement."

Tony looked at Mick for an answer.

"First, one or both parents might have a problem with a boy from a deeply religious Protestant family marrying an Italian Catholic girl. Second, Todd's old man wasn't presiding over the ceremony in his own church."

He nodded, turned his attention toward the screen again and said, "Well, let's get started finding this Rossi family, if any are still alive, who might lead us to Todd's ex."

"Whoa, Tony. Look at the time." It was already almost 11:30 p.m. "You should know, Mr. Morelli, if you call and awaken some aging Italian people right now, you might be burning another family bridge that might connect you to the mystery of Todd Kenilworth."

"You're right, Mick," he said, and was down the stairs and on Rush Street without even a "good night, buddy."

"He's hooked," Mick said, smiled and shut down his computer.

*****

Finding a Mario or Angelina Rossi in South Bend, Indiana wasn't like tracking down James or Mary Smith in New York City, so Tony called the only Angelina Rossi in the South Bend White Pages online Saturday afternoon.

"Mrs. Angelina Rossi?"

"Yes, who is this?"

"Hello, I'm Tony Morelli from Interstate Life Insurance. May I please speak with Lou Anne?"

"Lou Anne no live here no more. What you want?" said Mrs. Rossi through a lasagna-thick Italian accent.

"*Mi scusi, signora.* We've been trying to locate her. It seems her late husband had a small life insurance policy, and since his tragic death, *mi dispiace*, we might have some money for her."

"Wait."

The receiver clanked as if set on a hard surface. After a few minutes her voice returned above the shuffling of paper.

"You call her at 219 232-1415."

"Grazie, signora. Is this number—"

She hung up.

Tony recognized that the area code differed from Angelina Rossi's, 574, and called it.

"Come On Inn," said a male voice with the rasp of gravel on the other end. The collage of chatter, televised baseball, jukebox music and glass clatter told Tony he had called either a bar or a restaurant.

"Could I please speak with Lou Anne?"

"She isn't here right now." Without asking Tony who he was or what he wanted, the voice called away from the receiver, "Hey, Janie, Lou Anne coming in today?"

An inaudible far off voice replied.

"She'll be in around eight tonight until closing," the voice said back into the receiver.

"Thanks," Tony said and hung up. He didn't want to arouse any suspicions, so he didn't ask any questions. He had enough information to research Come On Inn.

Googling revealed that Come On Inn was a little bar in the unincorporated area called Fish Lake, Indiana, not far from South Bend and La Porte.

"You've just won an all-expense-paid, one night vacation to Fish Lake, Indiana, including complimentary cocktails at world renowned Come On Inn," said Tony when Mick picked up his home phone in Naperville.

"What?"

"I found Lou Anne. She's either a barfly, bartender or owner of this place a couple hours from here. Figured we could solve that mystery and maybe the Todd Kenilworth mystery, get hammered and stay in nearby La Porte or South Bend."

"Sorry, pal. I've got a date with an Angelina Jolie lookalike."

"How can I compete with your weekend? Let's see you signed John Grisham on Friday and you're going out with Angelina Jolie tonight. What are you doing tomorrow? Golfing with the President?"

"Had to call that off. I have other plans, but good luck with the mysteries."

They ended the conversation, and Mick turned the volume back up on the TV; the Cubs were winning.

*****

Tony had to feel lucky that Saturday night—lucky that he had a loving girlfriend who had bought him a beautiful car with a GPS system, lucky he had a friend like Mick to show him how to use it and lucky the GPS even knew about Fish Lake, let alone a little bar called Come On Inn. Most Indiana state maps didn't even mention the unincorporated community. Three connecting small bodies of water made up the protected waters called Fish Lake, linked by a channel that ran below

State Road 4. Come On Inn sat on a hill overlooking Lower Fish Lake on County Road 800.

He parked his Grand Cherokee among the line of pickup trucks and late model cars and walked into the frame ranch style establishment with the neon sign in the window, flashing Come On Inn. It seemed to Tony as if there were too few people for so many trucks. Two guys in tank tops, shorts and camouflage baseball caps played pool to the right. A couple of empty tables, a ceiling high TV screen and jukebox occupied the left side.

Three men around Tony's age sat at the L-shaped bar in front and the faint sound of men and women laughing, talking and singing in a room beyond the bar echoed toward the front. Everyone stopped what they were doing and looked at Tony standing just inside the door.

Tony felt as if he were burglar caught breaking into a home while the family sat staring at him in the living room. His expression must have reflected his sentiment because one guy at the bar raised his bottle of Miller Lite and said, "Yep, you're right. This isn't Chicago. Come on in!"

Everyone in the place, including Tony, laughed. He took a seat next to the guy who spoke and said, "How did you know I was from Chicago?"

"You've got that Chicago look about you. No, I just guessed, but don't feel out of place. Actually two out of three of us are originally from Chicago."

"What can I get you?" asked the bartender. She had Italian-like features, long dark hair and olive tanned skin, but she looked far too young, maybe in her early thirties, to be Todd's first wife.

"How about a Bud on tap?" Tony asked. He knew a small local tavern likely wouldn't have hefeweisen beer either in draft or bottles. "And how about a round for my three new friends?"

The guy at the end who wore a White Sox cap with a slight cock to the side raised his glass of red wine and said, "Long live Chi-town."

"That's Bill Walker, retired Chicago cop. This guy sitting next to me is Tim. He's the odd one, actually from the Fish Lake area, and I'm Henry. I used to work for a Chicago suburban school district."

It was Tony's turn. He decided to drop the insurance man guise and try honesty; these guys deserved it.

"My name's Tony Morelli. Actually, I came to talk to Lou Anne. I was a friend of her husband."

"Mike?" asked Henry.

"No, I meant her first husband, Todd."

"Don't know anything about him. She and Mike married a little over a year ago and bought this place. Former owners were having money problems."

"We three had thought about buying it," Bill said.

"Can you imagine us three guys running this place?" added Tim.

"It'd be like three monkeys trying to fuck a football," Henry said and gulped the last of his Miller Lite.

The door opened.

Tim turned and said, "There's Lou Ann now. Hey, Lou Anne, this guy came from Chicago to talk to you."

No one seems to look like I picture them, thought Tony. After talking to her mother, he imagined striking Italian features. Lou Anne's fair skin and long grayish blond hair accented the bright blueness of her eyes. She wore no make-up, but didn't need it. In a faded Notre Dame jersey and tight-fitting jeans she carried a bag of groceries behind the bar and into the kitchen.

About a minute later, she seemed to appear by magic sitting next to Tony. She wiped her hands with a bar rag and said, "Are you that insurance guy?"

Tony chuckled, choked a little on his beer, and said, "No, not exactly. Can we talk?"

She nodded toward the back room, and Tony followed her to a table secluded in the corner.

He knew this might be his last chance to get the story, if there was one, behind Todd Kenilworth's suicide. If Lou Anne slammed another door in his face, there were no more doors for him to knock on.

"Look, I'm telling you straight. My name's Tony Morelli. I'm not an insurance guy. I'm a writer and Todd was one of my childhood friends. This all started when I was on a book tour throughout Italy. I thought I encountered Todd after one of my talks in Palermo, Sicily."

He told her everything—from the punch to his jaw to the meetings with Beth and Laura.

Throughout his narration, Lou Anne stared expressionless at him. When he finished, she continued to stare. Tony couldn't interpret her look. Is she indifferent, enraged?

Tony could feel her penetrating glare as she stood up as if her chair were on fire. She grabbed Tony's heavy, thick beer mug within her clenched fist.

"You're going to need another beer, my friend," she said. "It's a long story, and I do think that was Todd you saw in Sicily."

She went behind the bar to pour him another draft.

THE RISE & "FALL" OF TODD KENILWORTH

Lou Anne returned with a frothing, misty mug of beer for Tony and white wine in a stemmed glass for herself. She sat down hard in her chair and sighed as if the drinks weighed a ton and said, "Where should I start?"

Tony wasn't sure whether she was asking him or herself, but he answered, "How about starting with how you and Todd met."

She gazed across the room at a table full of couples drinking and laughing and smiled.

Either her smile, her thoughts, or both make her look twenty years younger, thought Tony.

"It was at Terry and Laura's wedding," she said. "Terry and Rich DiFoggio are, were, my cousins."

"That's interesting," said Tony.

"You ain't heard nothing, yet," she said and sipped her wine. "Anyway, I thought he was cute. He walked up to me, and I could tell he was trying to hide his limp. He said, 'Believe it or not, I dance better than I walk.' I laughed, and we danced and talked the rest of the night. We dated for about a year. Todd was in law school at Chicago-Kent College. As soon as he finished law school and passed the bar, we got married."

She paused to sip her wine, and that youthful grin and faraway expression returned.

"Those were great years, the first few of our marriage," she continued. "Todd hooked up with a law firm at The Prudential Building in Chicago, Lulich & Goff."

"Pretty prestigious firm," said Tony, "but I thought they were in the suburbs, Orland Park?"

"They moved out there, later, like a lot of businesses and professionals. They followed the 'white flight' from the city to the suburbs. Plus taxes, rent, leases, everything was cheaper. Todd was making good money. I was teaching art at a nearby junior high school. We lived in a big house in Flossmoor near his dad's church. I hated teaching, and after a few years I quit. We didn't need the money, so I concentrated on my painting."

She raised her glass in the direction of some framed paintings, sandy beach landscapes on a paneled wall.

"Beautiful," said Tony

Her girlish smile disintegrated when she said, "Then it all seemed to deteriorate when my Uncle Frankie died."

Tony chugged the last of his beer and flashed a quizzical expression at Lou Anne.

"Frank DiFoggio. DiFoggio Construction," she answered his look.

"Oh, yeah," said Tony feeling the effects of the beer. "Who from Chicago doesn't know about DiFoggio Construction and the. . . "

He stopped himself. *Had the beer made me go too far? Don't want to burn another bridge.*

But Lou Anne just laughed and finished, "their mob connections." Her face changed from jovial to serious. She leaned across the table and said, "What few people know is that DiFoggio Construction, under Uncle Frankie, was legit. After his death, Richie took over is when everything turned to shit."

"So, how does Todd fit into all this?"

"Here is where the story gets interesting, and you need another beer," she said and took his mug back to the bar.

She smiled when she placed the beer in front of Tony— not that same childlike smile like before. It was a crafty grin, as if she had a secret she had been dying to tell for years and now this was her chance.

Tony didn't hide his eagerness. "So, you said, 'Here is where the story gets interesting.' Go on."

"Richie asked Terry and Todd if they wanted to be partners in the business. Terry worked for an insurance agency in New York and had never liked the family business. Todd knew his law firm frowned on Richie's shady connections, but Richie could be very persuasive, and Terry and Todd shared the same weakness; they loved to gamble. So, they invested in

DiFoggio Construction but only agreed if they were listed as silent partners. Seems like their gambling paid off."

"So, they became silent partners in a successful construction venture," Tony said.

"Within a year, Richie secured the contract from Mayor Jane Byrne and the City of Chicago to extend the Blue Line subway from downtown to O'Hare Airport. From city tax revenues to bank loans the contract amounted to over thirteen million dollars. Shortly after the work started, Richie declared DiFoggio Construction bankrupt.

"Naturally, the feds got suspicious. Their investigation led them to the theory that Richie skimmed most of the funds and paid huge sums to the mob, some politicians and himself. They had little proof of their theory, but had a strong case against Richie for felony fraud and tax evasion. He stood to do some serious jail time. Rumor had it that he had made a deal with the feds—immunity for his testimony that named mob figures and politicians who accepted skimmed funds."

"Every Chicagoan, as Paul Harvey used to say, 'knows the rest of the story,' " Tony mimicked the famous announcer's voice and then continued in his own, "The day before he was to testify before a grand jury, his bullet-ridden body was found at the Blue Line construction site with a dead canary in his mouth, and so the story ended."

"Not exactly. They never recovered the money, amounting to about ten million. Everyone assumed the mob had it hidden somewhere in untraceable cash. The city hired another construction company to finish the Blue Line and the mystery of who killed Richie and the missing money went cold.

"That's about the time our marriage got cold, too. Todd got very distant. His gambling habit got worse. He lied about being on business trips for the law firm. I thought he was having an affair until I tracked him down and discovered he had been visiting his sister and brother-in-law in New York. When I asked him about it, he got verbally abusive and told me to stay out of family business. Then, Terry . . ." she paused and gasped. Her words seemed to choke her.

Tony touched her hand as if it might break and said, "I know about his tragic death during the 9/11 attack."

Lou Anne exhaled and continued, "Laura moved back to Chicago, actually Tinley Park, about a year after Terry's death. I thought things would get better between Todd and me with his sister closer now, but tensions just got worse. Lulich & Goff passed over Todd for partnership. Todd got mad and quit the law firm. He decided to start his own practice of real estate law, but the sagging housing market made it difficult."

The bar had been getting more and more crowded. She scanned the customers, fielded some "Hey, Lou Annes" and then turned back toward Tony. She squinted into her empty wine glass as if she were searching for her next words.

"I suppose I was as much to blame for our break up. I got used to living comfortably and hounded him about our money problems."

Tony recalled Laura's words, "When Tony called her on her heavy spending, she'd berate him and call him 'cheap.'"

"We talked about divorce. That's funny and ironic," she said and chuckled. "Talking about divorce seemed to bring us closer together. We held it together for a few more years before departing amicably."

Tony snickered. He empathized with the humor and irony. He and his ex- had had similar divorce discussions. But he also noted the contradiction with Laura's account of the breakup.

"Anyway, it was an ugly divorce. Todd was really broken up. Okay, when I tell you this last part, let me see if you draw the same conclusion as I did. Todd's father was terminally ill. We agreed to hold off the divorce or even talk about it while he was alive. Todd and he were very close, and I loved the Rev, as I called him. Our divorce would have upset him terribly. So, for the next few years we held it together. Just before he died, The Chicago Tribune did a feature section in memory of the five year anniversary of the 9/11 attack. One story memorialized victims who had Chicago roots."

Tony held up his hand as he drank from his mug, and then said, "Wait a minute. Let me keep everything straight. Terry and Laura lived in New York. After Terry's death in 9/11, Laura moved back to Chicago—"

"With her baby daughter, Rebecca," Lou Anne corrected him, "and when the reporter wrote the story about 9/11 victims from Chicago, the name, Terry DiFoggio, must have rung a bell. He researched the DiFoggio construction scandal and some old corporate papers surfaced. Terry and Todd's names appeared as former business partners. The reporter called Todd and asked for a comment. Todd refused, and the reporter never wrote the story.

"Somehow, however, Todd's name on those corporate documents must have leaked out. We started getting threatening phone calls. The callers always asked, "Where's the money?" A week before our divorce became final, we sold the house and split the cash. Todd moved in with Laura and Rebecca, and I moved in with my mom in South Bend. I met Mike, my current husband, at Mom's church. We hit it off, eventually married and bought this place.

"Sorry, I'm getting ahead of myself; Todd and I met at my attorney's office to sign the final divorce papers. My attorney had a package that had been addressed to us. The new owners of our former house turned it over to their real estate agent who turned it over to my attorney. It was a dead canary with a dollar bill in its beak.

"The next day Laura, Rebecca, and Todd just disappeared. Two weeks later, the news hit about Todd's death in Rome. If I remember right, Laura's explanation to the press was something like, 'Todd was despondent over our divorce, his dad's death, his mom in a nursing home. They took the trip to cheer him up. It didn't work, blah, blah, blah,' all bullshit."

Laura pushed her wine glass aside, crossed her arms on the table and said, "Now, put together what you found out with my story. What do you think happened?"

Even though Tony's brain had become somewhat beer-soaked, he had been connecting the dots throughout Lou Anne's narrative. He clenched his beer mug, leaned closer to Lou Anne and said, "Either the mob caught up with him, Tony couldn't or wouldn't produce the missing ten million, so they whacked him, making it look like suicide—or. . ."

"Yes, or?" asked Lou Anne like a teacher trying to get her student to come up with an answer on his own.

"Or," the beer in Tony's brain seemed to evaporate. The fog in his head lifted, and he said, "Todd and Terry had hidden the money in a foreign bank. Tony faked his own death, and now lives off the ten million."

Lou Anne smiled at her astute pupil.

"Which theory do you think is true?" asked Tony.

"After hearing what you told me about your encounter in Italy and your visits to the old lady at the nursing home and Laura, I know the answer."

Tony just squinted at her.

"It's definitely the second theory. Todd's alive; that was him you saw in Sicily."

"How can you be so sure?"

"Remember you said when you visited the old lady—sorry, Beth—she thought Todd was alive in Italy and phoned her off and on."

"Yeah, but that could still be Laura somehow faking it, so she doesn't upset her mother in her fragile state."

"You said just before leaving you told her, 'If I see Todd, I'll say that his mother's doing fine here at Peace Valley, or something to that effect. Right?"

"Sure, but I was just trying to appease her belief in the charade."

"What was her response, again?"

"She's obviously senile or suffers from some kind of dementia, because she got all upset and said, 'Todd's mother isn't a frail old woman in a nursing home!' "

"Beth was right. Todd's real mother lives in Italy."

The beer mug slipped through Tony's hands.

MAMA MIA

Tony followed Lou Anne to the back. She fumbled with her keys and unlocked the sliding glass patio doors. They both stepped outside and onto the wooden deck far above the lake below. She closed the door and locked out the noise, and a voice called, "Hey, let us come out there, too!"

Lou Anne just laughed and joined Tony, who looked out across the dark mirror-like lake that reflected the lights from a few pontoon boats and lakeside cottages.

"Why don't you let some of that crowd spill out here?" asked Tony. "It's beautiful."

"Oh, we tried that earlier this summer. It's too enticing for drunks. Some idiot thought he was Spider Man and dove off this railing. Damn near broke his neck. It's only about four feet deep right down there. During the day and on less crowded nights we keep it open."

They both stared at the glimmering reflections off the water. Tony broke the silence and said, "Okay, forgive me if I seem a little dense, but between the beer and the long story I need to get this all straight.

"Terry and Laura got married. You and Todd met at their wedding. Terry is your cousin. Terry's brother Rich brings Terry and Todd, your husband, into the family business, DiFoggio Construction, as silent partners. The company lands a big contract with the city of Chicago. Rich skims huge sums of money for the project so he can pay off politicians and the mob, but before these crooks get their cut, Rich declares bankruptcy. The mob has him killed, but millions are still missing. Terry and Todd may have recovered the money, but the mob doesn't know this because they are 'silent partners.' Terry dies during 9/11.

"In the aftermath, a story about the victims leaks to the mob that Terry and Todd were part of the business. Scared that the mob is after him, Todd fakes his own death to get the gangsters off his back and, maybe, now lives off the skimmed millions in Italy. So, you said Todd's real mother was in Italy, and I dropped my mug."

She smiled but continued to gaze at the lake as if she were in a trance. "Yes. A few weeks after the Rev's funeral, Todd and I decided to tell Beth about our breaking up. She seemed to have recovered well and was ready to hear it, but when we got to her house we changed our minds. She was in a melancholy mood. She asked Todd and me if we would go up into her attic and go through his father's stored belongings. She couldn't. She said, 'Take what you want and throw out the rest. I can't handle it.'

"Most of it was crap. At least I thought it was crap. Old army issued stuff: backpack, canteen, mess kit. To Todd it was treasure. He was kind of a pack rat. If we weren't divorcing we'd be arguing about what to throw out and what to keep, but I figured it was all his decision now. That's when I came across a beat-up leather satchel with documents inside. It included army discharge papers, letters from Todd's grandparents to his dad, and a photo copy of a document written in Italian. 'I wonder what this is,' I said and handed it to him.

"For reasons unknown to me and even to Todd, Todd had always had an interest in Italian culture. He even took courses, whenever he had time, to learn the language—just for fun. He mouthed as he read, translated silently and held the document near the hanging single light bulb. 'My God,' he said. 'It's a birth certificate.' I took it from his hands and looked at it. You didn't have to be an expert in Italian to translate the date; it was the same as Todd's birthday.

"He grabbed it from me and bolted down the ladder. 'Wait!' I yelled to him. 'Not now! She's still mourning.' I knew he was going to confront Beth. 'I don't care,' he yelled back. 'I've got to know.' I just stood next to that bulb, closed my eyes and listened. First, there was a low murmur of voices, and then the explosion. Beth shrieked. All I remember are the words: 'No! No! Not now! Not after all this time! Why God, did you let him find out?'"

Lou Anne's shoulders shook as she spoke.

Tony touched her forearm resting on the railing until she stopped shaking.

"Thank you," she said and continued, "I ran down the steps and put my arms around Beth seated on the couch. She sobbed uncontrollably. I gave Todd a dirty look, and he went to the kitchen and returned with a glass of water. I handed her the glass. As she sipped it, she seemed to calm down. Todd sat across from us.

"As much as he wanted answers, I think he realized that bringing this up so soon after his father's death was a bad idea. 'Sorry, sorry, ma. I shouldn't have—' but she waved off his apology. 'No, no,' she said, 'it's my. . . I mean our fault. Your father and I should have told you long ago. I guess we thought it didn't matter if you knew or not. It didn't matter to us, but you deserve to know the truth.' She took a long drink of water and set it on the coffee table. I don't remember her words verbatim, but essentially this is the story she told:

"She and the Rev met at Southern Methodist University. He was a theology major working on a doctorate in ministry, and she was an undergrad in the School of Business. They married right after he graduated and moved into an apartment in Dallas. She continued her studies at SMU.

"David, the Rev, enlisted in the army as a chaplain. He had felt guilty that his two older brothers had served in World War II; the oldest gave his life, but the Rev was too young. His parents wouldn't let him quit high school and join. The army assigned him to the "Stay Behind" project, a post-war program set up in coalition with NATO, the CIA and the Italian government in the 1950s.

"On paper, the mission was to help rebuild Italy after the war. In reality, it was a covert operation to discourage the spread of communism. The Communist Party, with the help of Russia, our former WWII ally, threatened to take over Italian municipalities and eventually the country. Do you remember something in the news, oh, maybe twenty or thirty years ago, of evidence coming to light of U.S. involvement in false flag bombings in Europe during the Cold War of the 50s?"

Tony closed his eyes like a kid in class trying to remember an answer on a test. He nodded his head and said, "Vaguely, something about proof that Western European terrorist groups actually planted bombs in their own communities before elections, and the U.S. somehow helped them?"

"Helped them blame it on the Russian Communist Party," Lou Anne finished for him. "Beth never knew if her husband knew about all this while he was stationed there. His job as chaplain was to provide spiritual support for the troops and comfort to both Italian and American victims of the bombings.

"During his three-year stint, David took several leaves. He and Beth would meet in New York for short romantic interludes. Beth got pregnant and gave birth to Laura a year before the army honorably discharged the Rev with glowing recommendations. He returned to Dallas . . . with a three-month old baby boy.

"His story was simple. After a village bombing, he visited survivors in a hospital. One was a prostitute who delivered the baby while recuperating from burns. The father of the child was killed in the bombing. She begged David to take her son to America for a better chance at life. She threatened to take both hers and the baby's lives if he didn't.

"According to David, some high-ranking officers revered the deeds of chaplains more than any other military personnel. With the help of such officers, strings were pulled, papers were signed, and the Kenilworths eventually left Dallas for a life in Chicago with their son, Todd, and two-year old daughter."

"Okay," said Tony, "that explains the Mediterranean-looking Todd in the otherwise pale-skinned Kenilworth clan, but it doesn't tell me how you know his mother is still alive in Italy."

"That's the most interesting part. It's the last detail that I can tell you about the secret life of Todd Kenilworth. Todd had been listening stoically throughout Beth's entire story—almost as if he had suspected something like this all his life. It wasn't until after she returned from her bedroom with a locked wood-carved jewelry box that Todd finally reacted. She unlocked it, handed the key and the box to him and said, 'These are yours now.' I stood next to him. He opened each envelope, one-by-one. They were birthday cards from his mother in Italy for every one of Todd's birthdays, from his first to his most recent. The box and cards dropped to the floor when he put his hands over his face and cried like a baby."

LETHAL SHOCK

A scratching sound coming from the kitchen awakened Tony early Monday morning. He had planned on sleeping until the afternoon and picking up Pauline at the airport that evening.

After hearing Lou Anne's story Saturday night, the guys he had met at Come On Inn refused to let him leave without letting them buy him drinks. The four of them closed the bar at 4 a.m. Lou Anne and Mike refused to let Tony drive to a motel, so he slept in the guest room of their house down the street. He spent Sunday in his apartment nursing a hangover, watching the Cubs drop a doubleheader to the Cardinals and thinking about Todd Kenilworth. Did he really steal ten million dollars from the mob, fake his own death and hide out in Italy? Is there enough for a story here that I can use for a book? If so, where do I go from here? Italy? Where in Italy?

His most immediate mystery involved the scratching sound in the kitchen. He put on his robe and walked from his bedroom, through the living room and toward the kitchen. With every step the source of the strange scuffing became clearer. It wasn't coming from the kitchen, but rather the apartment door off the kitchen, and the scratching was really the clicking sound of someone trying to work the lock. Before Tony could react to the apparent break in, the door flew open.

"Don't shoot. I got an early flight and decided to surprise you."

Tony sighed, laughed and said, "Damn, Pauline, you scared the shit out of me."

They embraced in the hallway. Tony's robe fell to the floor much to the distaste of Mrs. Cornwall retrieving her Chicago Sun-Times outside her door across the hall. Pauline's warm curvy body and rose-scented red hair made him forget all about everything—Todd Kenilworth, Mrs. Cornwall's screech, even writing. He was as much in love with her, maybe more, as he was when they first met in Italy years earlier. They had talked about marriage in the recent past, but both balked at the commitment, only because of their past failures at matrimony. Tony revered her love of performing her music, and she respected his passion for writing; however, if Pauline had asked him to quit writing for her, he knew he'd do it in a heartbeat. No one in Tony's life ever held that power.

In the bedroom, they made love like two horny college kids on spring break. Afterward, Tony let Pauline sleep off some of her jet lag while he showered, got dressed and made coffee. He spent the next hour and a half sitting on the couch and dividing his time between reading the newspaper, watching Morning Joe on MSNBC and sipping his coffee.

He walked to the window and admired his fire engine red Jeep parked across the street, beneath the shade of an old oak tree and a younger maple growing in the parkway.

"Like my anniversary gift to you?"

Pauline, fully dressed, stood in the hallway leading from the bedroom to the living room.

"Love it," said Tony, "but like Mick and I decided when we drove it home from the airport, I don't deserve it. Besides, I haven't given you your present yet. Can you wait?"

She half closed her eyes, put on her little-girl-mischievous smile, sauntered toward him and planted a passionate kiss on his lips. In a low, whispering voice she said, "I can wait forever, and you know you really don't have to get me anything."

Tony closed his eyes. Her sincerity almost made him feel embarrassed.

"Now," she said like a stern school teacher breaking the mood, "give me the keys to your new buggy. I paid for it; I get to drive it."

Tony threw her the keys and said, "What's mine is yours, but don't you want to sleep some more? Jet lag must have your days and nights totally screwed up."

"No, no, no. There's only one cure for jet lag, and that's staying awake until night in your current time zone, then crash. I've got plans to meet my friend, Janet, for lunch at Eataly downtown, and then we're going on a serious shopping spree at Water Tower Place until it gets dark."

"Knock yourself out. I'm working on a new project that I'll tell you about when you have more time."

"You better," she said and slammed the door behind her.

Tony sipped from his coffee cup. The coffee, now cold, still tasted good. *Life is good*, he thought. When he exhaled and plopped back down on the couch, it seemed as if all his problems and worries transferred from his body and brain and into those soft cushions and finally vanished.

That's when it hit—a boom from outside that shook the building. He turned toward the window. Flames and smoke shot through the branches and leaves of the oak and maple trees. He knew his Jeep had exploded.

"PAULINE!"

His empty cup fell onto the rug, and he ran to the door.

PRIME SUSPECT

His once beautiful SUV looked like a melting plastic toy. Flames shot from the interior and undercarriage and licked the blackening, liquefying metal exterior. Tony imagined Pauline's lifeless body swallowed in the flames. His body quaked, and nausea overtook him. He fell to his knees on the parkway grass. The thought of her gone choked him, and an urge to join her brought him to his feet.

A small group gathered on Tony's side of the street and focused on something lying on the curb. Tony forgot his queasiness and fought through the mass. Pauline lay on the curb. Two people kneeled and spoke encouragement: "You'll be okay. Help is on the way."

He pushed them away and said, "Pauline, it's Tony. Can you hear me?"

Her entire front—hair, eyebrows, and clothes—singed or burned a charcoal black/gray. She turned her head toward him and half opened her eyes. Her lips moved, but no words came out. She opened her fist, and the key fob fell to the street.

"Remote, she's trying to say," someone said. "I think she's telling us that starting the car with the remote set the explosion, probably saved her life."

The paramedics moved in. Tony didn't even remember hearing sirens. Within seconds they assessed her vital signs, put an oxygen mask on her and whisked her onto a backboard and into the ambulance. Tony jumped inside it with her.

"Who are you?" asked a paramedic.

"Husband," Tony lied. "Where are we going?"

"Loyola Hospital in Maywood."

"Rush Oak Park is practically around the corner," said Tony as if the young emergency worker were a disobedient child.

"Loyola has one of the best burn units in the country. Don't worry, sir. We'll be there in seconds. We know what we're doing," he said and closed the double ambulance doors.

Tony held her hand as the vehicle weaved through traffic yielding to the whining siren. He badgered his brain with questions: *Who would do this? That bomb was meant for me, so why her? What would have happened if she hadn't used the remote start? Why would someone do this?* "Don't leave me, Pauline."

An emergency team met the ambulance at the hospital. Tony followed them as they wheeled Pauline's gurney into a huge room with curtained stations. A security guard stopped him as doctors and nurses rolled her into one and closed the curtains.

Before Tony could protest, a kind looking middle-aged woman wearing a surgical smock and carrying a clipboard said, "Are you with her?"

"Yes."

"Don't worry. She's getting the best attention right now. Please come with me; I need to get some information."

The next twenty-five minutes seemed like hours to Tony. He answered questions about Pauline: her health, insurance, family, and so forth. When he finished, the admittance attendant told him to have a seat in the Emergency Room Waiting Area, but he had made up his mind to find Pauline; however, two Oak Park Police Officers met him as soon as he stood up.

"Mr. Morelli?" one cop asked.

"Yes."

"We'd like you to come with us and answer some questions."

A doctor came through the double swinging emergency room doors. Tony recognized him from the curtained station, ignored the cops and approached him.

"How is Pauline?"

The doctor paused a moment and asked, "Are you the husband?"

"Yes," he lied again.

"Well, I can tell you that her exterior burns are very superficial. She is lucky. At the same time, she inhaled a lot of smoke and heat. She is showing signs of bronchospasms and edema which is not uncommon with these cases."

"Speak English, Doctor."

"Her throat and larynx have swelled making breathing and speaking difficult."

"Will she be okay? Will she be able to speak? Sing? She's a singer, you know."

The doctor's facial expression gave no clue to an answer. "Look, her vital signs are very good. I am optimistic about her recovery, but the next twenty-four to forty-eight hours will tell. Included in her tests will be a bronchoscopy and laryngoscopy. The results will give us a clearer picture of the extent of damage, if any, to her vocal chords.

Right now she needs rest, oxygen and fluids for the next few days while we conduct tests. Even if she could speak, we don't want her using her voice for at least a couple of days. You need to go home and relax. Give her a full day tomorrow with no visitors, so we can run tests, and she can recover quietly."

*****

Tony sat alone in a room at the Oak Park Police station. It was a typical interrogation room, right out of a cop TV series—small, sterile, bright fluorescent ceiling light, three plastic-back chairs, four-foot cheap folding table, two-way mirror on one wall, video lens with a tiny red dot light tucked in the upper corner, and even a plastic-lined puke basket for nervous interviewees.

An aficionado of the true crime cable channels, Tony knew the routine. They would watch him from the adjacent room through the two-way mirror to see if he acted suspiciously or made any phone calls on his cell. When they got sufficiently bored, they would begin questioning him. Tony was as anxious to find out who planted the bomb as they were. He also knew that being the owner and survivor of the bombed Jeep made him a prime suspect. He did his best to bore them.

After a few minutes two plainclothes detectives entered the room. Both wore dress shirts, plain ties, suit pants, but no jackets. The younger one looked like a college linebacker. He had a pock-marked face, a crew-cut and carried a pen and legal pad. The middle-aged cop had groomed, slicked back brown hair. His stubble and rolled up sleeves gave the impression of a frustrated cop who's been working all night.

Let's see, who's the good cop and who's the bad cop? I'm betting the older guy's the bad cop, Tony thought.

He was wrong.

"Sorry about this, Mr. Morelli," said the older cop. "We know you're upset about your vehicle and your . . . is she your girlfriend, wife?"

"Girlfriend."

"But we need some questions answered—"

"And you can spare us any bullshit, please," interrupted linebacker cop as he sat down and slapped his legal pad on the table.

The older cop held up his palms toward him and nodded as if to say, "Calm down, I'll handle this."

They've got their routine down pat, Tony mused.

"I'm Lieutenant Bianco and this is Detective Kaminski."

Kaminski didn't look up; he just wrote on his pad.

"Let's start by you telling us what events led up to the bombing of your car and your girlfriend's injuries," said Bianco.

Tony began with his returning from Italy and receiving his gift of the Jeep at the airport. He said he had spent the weekend working on research for another book and it ended with Pauline's surprise arrival and the bombing.

Bianco asked him personal questions about his prior marriage, his work and finally Pauline.

"How would you describe your relationship with Pauline?" asked Bianca.

"Excellent," said Tony.

"Yeah, we've heard that before," said Kaminski, "usually right after we've identified the girlfriend's corpse."

Tony knew Kaminski was trying to piss him off, to catch him off balance, and to make him say something that might lead to a confession. But Tony kept his cool.

After about fifteen minutes of this line of questioning, Tony said, "Look, I know you guys have to look at me first as a prime suspect, but believe me, I want to find out who did this more than you do, so let's cut-to-the-chase. Hook me up to a polygraph or whatever else you have to do, but let's move on and find the son-of-a-bitch who did this."

Kaminski stopped writing, and the two cops stared at each other.

"You'd agree to a polygraph test?" asked Bianco.

"Anything."

"Okay, that can be arranged, but it'll have to be later tonight when our lie detector expert is due in. In the meantime, Mr. Morelli, who would benefit or want to see you dead?"

The direction of the interrogation changed. Questions focused on his former wife, the divorce, his past writings, and then his present project. In all the emotion and commotions of the day, it hadn't occurred to Tony that there might be a connection with this Todd Kenilworth venture and the bombing. His recent research involved angry family members and even the mob.

Before he could share any of this, a uniformed cop entered and said, "Excuse me, could I talk to you two guys for a minute?"

The two cops left and shut the door.

After over an hour, Kaminski and Bianco returned. This time Kaminski looked at Tony and not just his notes. It was obvious to Tony that both cops wanted to see Tony's reaction when Bianco said, "We got the guy who planted the bomb."

Tony looked at the ceiling, exhaled, slapped his palms on the table and said, "Thank God."

THE MAD BOMBER

"You know this guy?" said Kaminski. He had pulled a computer-generated printout of a mug shot from the top of his legal pad and handed it to Tony.

Tony scrutinized the profile and frontal shot like a Wheel of Fortune contestant trying to solve a puzzle, but nothing about the guy looked familiar. The subject looked to be in his early forties or late thirties with a fat face, brown hair slicked back into a short ponytail, and a goatee. His indifferent expression made Tony think, *this guy's no stranger to the mug shot camera.*

"Who is he?" asked Tony shaking his head and returning the sheet.

"Small-time criminal named Nicky Altobelli," answered Bianco, "also known as 'the mad bomber.'"

Both detectives snickered when Bianco finished.

"What's so funny?" asked Tony.

Kaminski dropped the bad cop attitude and said, "Sorry, the 'mad bomber' nickname is kind of a joke. Altobelli has been a mob wannabe all his life. Problem is the mob wants nothing to do with him. He's careless and not the sharpest knife in the drawer as they say—usually gets caught. In this case, one of your neighbors walking his dog last night saw a guy dressed in a black hoody crawl out from beneath your car.

"We identified him minutes later on a mini-mart surveillance footage buying a Twinkie and a can of beer. He started his life of crime as a kid helping a guy tow illegally parked cars in Chicago to his private lot and then extorting money from the owners to get their vehicles back."

"Cassio and The Lincoln Park Pirates?" asked Tony.

"I guess you are a genuine Chi-town boy," said Kaminski. "Everyone from Chicago knows about Cassio from the Steve Goodman song. Altobelli moved on to arson and warning bombs, bombs set off when no one's around so no one gets hurt or killed—just to send a message like 'pay up, bug off, or don't testify.' Anyone want to send you any of those messages?"

Tony thought about Laura and Todd (if he was truly still alive), but decided to keep quiet. He wasn't sure why. Maybe he thought the cops wouldn't believe, or worse, they would believe him and botch up his chance for good story. He was sure of one thing, and shared this with Kaminski and Bianco,

"Whoever hired him, assuming someone hired him, wasn't sending me a message. They or he or she wanted me dead. No one could have known Pauline wanted to test drive my new car. Even I didn't expect it, and no one could have expected she'd use the remote start. Did you question this guy?"

Both looked down.

"He lawyered up," said Bianco.

"Can I talk to him?"

"Wish you could," said Kaminski, "but he's on his way back to Danville Correctional. This arrest also means he violated his parole on a weapons charge. Besides, Tony . . . can I call you Tony?"

Tony nodded.

"He's not going to tell you anything. His knowledge about who hired him is a trump card for him and his attorney. If he wants to talk, they'll use what he knows to try and strike a deal with the prosecutor."

A dead silence settled in the room.

"My life might still be in danger, right?"

Neither Kaminski nor Bianco responded right away.

"Maybe," Bianco said, "and maybe not. Whoever is behind this knows the heat's on now and seeing you dead may not be worth the risk of getting caught, especially if they have little to gain by your death except vengeance. Actually, I'll bet Altobelli is in more danger, even in prison, if someone's afraid he'll talk."

"Look we'll keep a watch on your house and you for a while until something breaks. In the meantime," Kaminski said and looked at his watch, "Watson, the polygraph guy, will be on duty in about an hour. Would you mind hanging around until then, just so we can eliminate you as a suspect and tie up some loose ends?"

"Why not?" said Tony. He felt and looked drained.

Kaminski put a hand on Tony's shoulder and led him outside the room. "Come on," he said, "I'll take you to our break room and buy you some coffee. You hungry?"

Tony shook his head and followed him to an open area with vending machines, a kitchen and several folding tables and chairs. He took a seat at a vacant table while Kaminski brought him a cup of coffee from the machine.

"I'll be leaving soon, but I'll leave word for Watson to find you here when he checks in," said Kaminski and left.

An overweight uniformed cop who looked like he should have retired ten years earlier ignored Tony and read from the only newspaper at another table.

Bored, Tony tried to read the front page as the cop held it open and read an inside story. The headline read: RAPIST SUSPECT'S LAWYER SEEKS MISTRIAL.

Tony grabbed his coffee and ran to find Kaminski or Bianco. Bianco stood up from his desk, larger and set apart from the others, put on his suit coat and looked as if he were leaving for the day.

"Lieutenant?" Tony said and approached him. When he got close enough so no else could hear he continued, "Could I look at this Mad Bomber's file?"

"No, but why would you want to do that?"

"Maybe there's something or someone in there that connects this guy to me that I'm unaware of."

Bianco raised his eyebrows and smiled. "Might be a good idea if you were allowed to read his file," he nodded toward a thick legal-sized file folder lying next to his shut down computer. The label on the file tab read: ALTOBELLI, NICHOLAS. "Tell you what," he said loud enough for others to hear. "Finish your coffee right here at my desk," and then whispered to Tony, "and make sure everything seems in order because that file goes to the prosecutor's office tomorrow morning." He winked and left.

Tony pulled the cushy chair closer to the desk and opened the file. It was full of pictures, court documents, and letters arranged chronologically from top to bottom—earliest records on top. Toward the bottom he found it, a letter from Altobelli's attorney to a Cook County assistant prosecutor. It had something to do with Altobelli wanting to plead guilty to a Class 2 felony of arson rather than a more serious charge of aggravated arson; it didn't matter. The lawyer's signature mattered: Todd Kenilworth.

Tony sipped his coffee, still hot.

LIAR, LIAR

The seventh floor, the burn center, of Loyola University Hospital was a busy place Monday at about 10:30 a.m.—so busy that no one seemed to notice Tony waiting in Pauline's room for her to return from a series of tests. He had passed the polygraph test with flying colors the night before at the Oak Park P.D. It's a good thing he didn't have to take a lie detector test at the end of this day because he would have flunked it worse than Stevie Wonder taking a driver's test. He started by lying to the hospital staff and saying that since he was Pauline's husband the doctor said he could visit her between her tests that day.

Earlier that morning, he had made an insurance claim on the Jeep and picked up a rental car, part of his policy coverage. The unfortunate rental was a far cry from his plush Jeep. The only car available as per the limits of his policy was a Smart Fortwo, a car only inches larger than a household refrigerator for Tony's six-foot frame.

"Do I drive it or just wear it?" asked Tony.

A heavyset nurse, arms crossed and face contorted into a condescending frown, entered Pauline's room where Tony sat on her empty bed.

"Mr. Morelli," she said like an old maid high school math teacher who just caught Tony cheating on a test, "I just spoke with the doctor on the phone. You are not the husband, and you were not given permission to see her today."

"Ahh, I see the problem. You spoke to the wrong doctor. You see I—"

"No, no, no," she said and escorted him out of the room, "Dr. Fleming said to meet him in the Burn Center Conference Room at 9:30 tomorrow morning. He'll go over the results of all the testing with you, and then you can see her all you want. We'll tell her you came to visit her. Now please leave."

Tony drove to Laura Kenilworth DiFoggio's house. He would wait all day for her if she wasn't home. His plan: confront her about the connection between the Mad Bomber and her brother, share his suspicion that she hired Altobelli to blow up him and his car for getting too nosey, and threaten to take his suspicion to the police if she didn't have answers.

Another mild shock hit him when he turned off Harlem Avenue and drove toward the house. It was up for sale. Two rows of stuffed plastic garbage bags lined the curb the length of the building and an Anoman & Associates Real Estate sign was displayed on the front lawn. He parked in the driveway, stepped outside of his Smart car and stared at the sign in disbelief.

I was just in this place a few days ago. Usually there are signals that the people are moving: boxes, stacked articles. This had to be a last minute decision.

Tony pulled out his smart phone and Googled Anoman & Associates. The website's Meet Our Realtors page listed five agents. Tony picked the person who looked the most green and in need of a sale and called the number.

"Anoman and Associates, Allison Hanes speaking."

"Allison, my name is Tony Morelli. I happened to pass by one of your homes for sale and nearly crashed my little car. It's exactly what my wife and I are looking for in this neighborhood. I'm afraid I only have my lunch hour today to spare this week, but if it's what I think, our searching is over and I'll want to make an offer."

"Oh, my God . . . I mean, I can't. . . no wait. . . I'll be there within a half hour. Don't move."

"I'll be waiting and drooling here in the driveway," Tony said and hung up. "My second big lie of the day," he said to himself. "Hope she buys my act better than that nurse."

Allison parked her black Ford Escape behind his Smart Car.

"Mr. Molini?" she said and retrieved a file folder from her front seat. Her long blond hair, coed short skirt and perky personality gave the impression that this was her first real job after college."

"Morelli."

"Sorry, Mr. Morelli. Well, I can't tell you much about this place, sir. It just went on the market. All I know is that it's fully furnished and a great buy. These printouts just came out today," she said and handed a stapled packet to him from her folder.

Tony scanned the information.

"Wow, the price is really reasonable. What's the catch?"

"Owner's in a hurry to sell."

"Why?"

She ignored his question, and he followed her inside to the living room. It looked the same as it had a few days ago when he stood there. Even the big screen TV was left behind. The only thing missing was the family photo on the fireplace mantle. He looked through the picture window at the rows of bulging garbage bags. *They took only what fit in a car or a plane, and packed the rest in those bags or left it in the house.*

"I love it already," said Tony, and he repeated his enthusiasm everywhere she led him. By the time they finished the tour Allison must have thought he would write a check and expect her to hand him the keys.

"What do you think, Mr. Morelli?" she asked as they stood in the driveway.

Tony looked at the house and scrunched his face into a frown. "You know, Allison, I'd be willing to make an offer within an hour. I'd do it right now, but I'd have to talk with my wife first. But something bothers me."

"What?" Allison appeared as if she'd wet her panties with the excitement of making this sale.

"Well, I keep asking myself, 'Why would the owner want to sell this beautiful house at such a low price and apparently skip town?' There must be something wrong with it—termites, mice, maybe even rats. I don't know."

Allison skimmed the surroundings as if she were looking for hidden cameras. She stepped closer to Tony and said,

"Look, Mr. Morelli, if I, if anyone at Anoman & Associates had all the information about the owner I'd find out and tell you to make this sale. I'll tell you all I know."

She scrutinized the neighborhood again. "The owner said that she and her daughter had to leave the country on a family emergency. She wouldn't tell us where or give us any contact information, only that she would contact our agency weekly on the progress of the sale, and we should accept any reasonable offer. She would make the closing arrangements long distance. Between you and me, I think they were running from some kind of trouble that has nothing to do with this beautiful house."

"Why do you say that?"

"It was the way the woman acted. Actually, it was more the way her daughter acted. The girl made it clear that she didn't want to sell the house and move. I mean I could see why a kid wouldn't want to leave her friends at school and all, but even a kid wouldn't make such a fuss about leaving a house if it had bugs and critters. No, Mom wanted to skip town, not get rid of the house. I'm not even sure the kid knew why. Mr. Morelli, please don't say anything about what I just said. I could lose my job."

"Allison, how could you lose your job after making a sale from just one showing? Give me your card. You'll hear from me within an hour."

Tony felt guilty for instilling such exhilaration in her.

"Fantastic!" she said, gave him her card and just missed a parked car when she backed out of the driveway.

Tony's major concern? Get Allison the hell away, so he could discover where Laura and Rebecca DiFoggio had fled.

He approached the line of garbage bags.

PAULINE

A tall plastic blue recycling bin stood at the front of the line of garbage bags. Tony lifted the lid and sifted through the plastic bottles and tin cans. He grabbed a stack of discarded papers, closed the lid and sorted through them. Most of it amounted to junk mail and empty envelopes. One crumpled printout proved worthy of notice—a confirmation statement from Orbitz Travel for two one-way tickets to Rome on Alitalia Airlines departing on Sunday afternoon and reservations at the Eurostars International Palace Hotel Rome for one week.

One-way tickets and one-week reservations, Tony thought. Where are they headed from there?

He rummaged through the rest of the bin but found nothing of value, so he started ripping open the garbage bags. Most contained discarded clothes and linens. One looked as if the heavy contents had already poked through and stretched at the thin black plastic liner. Inside, Tony discovered a stack of framed pictures and photos including the one he had seen on the mantel and some empty jewelry boxes. His eyes widened.

The hand-carved wooden box that Lou Anne had described to him stood out among the jewelry boxes. He lifted it but couldn't tell whether or not it still contained the birthday cards from Todd's mother in Italy; it was locked and the key wasn't within the bag. He perused his rented Smart car and located the small tire iron in the emergency fix-it kit.

He popped open the box lid, and a stack of envelopes sprang out like a jack-in-the-box. The most recent postmark was only a year old. The return address read: Pier Sagona, 113 Via Ceccano, Frosinone, Italia 03100. He took the Orbitz confirmation document and the box of cards to his car. Wait a minute, he thought and went back to the torn bag of pictures and photos. He recovered the family photo from the mantel before heading back home.

As much as this mystery intrigued him, one concern prioritized everything—Pauline. He could not leave her now, and he didn't want to. It was probable that his snooping had led to the bombing, her injury and possibly the end of her singing career.

"Forget about Todd Kenilworth and all this nonsense, Tony," he said aloud as he drove,. But as much as he loved Pauline, he knew that he couldn't.

*****

The conference room at the hospital reminded Tony of his high school days. He was a smart student, average athlete, but couldn't resist being a wise ass in the classroom. Some teachers loved him, while others got hooked on aspirin or alcohol when they discovered Tony's name on their class rosters. He planted a recording of various farm animal sounds behind the air vent in the classroom of his pompous French teacher.

During one of her dull conjugation of verb lectures he activated the recorder with a remote device. She nearly went insane before one of her arrogant pet students snitched on Tony. He felt the same anxiety waiting for Dr. Fleming as he did waiting for the high school dean to show up and administer a punishment.

Dr. Fleming showed up at ten after ten for his 9:30 meeting with Tony. "Well, Mr. Morelli, I have some good news. Your girlfriend can go home today," he said as he closed the door behind him, took a seat at the head of the table and offered no apology for his tardiness, "and the results of the tests are good; however . . ."

"However?" Tony said in effort to break the doctor's suspicious pause.

"You mentioned that she was a singer?"

"Yes."

"Yesterday her voice was rather raspy and hoarse. The laryngoscopy showed some inflammation of the vocal cords, which is quite normal after breathing in some smoke and flames. The inflammation will clear up quickly. The reality is that we can't predict whether or not there is a permanent change to the voice box. It may return to normal; it may change with regard to vocal strength or range, or it may retain its hoarse quality that we heard yesterday."

"When will we know?"

"She's resting right now, but we may see some improvement as early as today or within few weeks. You can see her now. Please don't encourage her to talk very much. The less she talks, the faster she heals."

When Tony entered her room, she appeared to be sleeping. As he crept closer, her eyes opened. She looked angelic—hair combed out, her singed eyebrows and lashes touched-up, no other make-up, but she didn't need it to look glowing.

"Don't say anything," Tony said and held her hand as if it were breakable. "Let me speak. My lust for a good story is the reason you're lying here."

Pauline narrowed her penciled-on eyebrows into a confused expression.

"It all started in Palermo, when I called you after that guy tagged me, who I thought was someone from my childhood."

She nodded.

He told her the whole chain of events: visiting Todd's mother, getting thrown out of Laura's house, Todd's ex's story at Come On Inn, the Mad Bomber, the connection between the Mad Bomber and Todd, Laura's flight to Italy and Tony's suspicion that Laura and Todd arranged the bombing. At that point, his eyes welled.

His Sicilian heritage reminded him of that phony macho code, "Men of honor don't cry," but a tear formed and dribbled down his face. "Pauline, I love you. You buy me a beautiful automobile, and what do I do? I nearly get you killed, and your voice, your beautiful voice . . . I don't know what I can do or say now." He buried his face in his hands and wept.

Pauline sat up and grasped both of Tony's wrists and pulled him closer. She smiled at him as if she were looking at a hurt little boy and said in the same sonorous, melodious voice that Tony had always heard her use, either to speak or sing, "Go to Italy, and get that bitch."

PART II:

RITORNO A ROMA

STALKER

After taking Pauline back to the apartment, Tony contacted the Oak Park P.D. Lieutenant Bianco told him that the Mad Bomber still wasn't talking, so Tony shared his information about Laura and Todd's connection to him and about her fleeing to Italy.

"Great," said Bianco. "We'll feed this information to the prosecutor. Maybe he can get the Bomber's attorney to get him to talk. If that happens, we'll get a warrant for her arrest and begin extradition procedures with the Italian police. In the meantime, sit tight."

Tony wasn't hearing Bianco's advice. Laura's reservations at Eurostars International Palace Hotel Rome lasted only until the end of the week. Knowing how slow the wheels of justice grind, he planned to book a room across the street from her hotel and stalk her until he knew where she planned to settle. If the Mad Bomber fingered her, and maybe even Todd, he could help the Italian authorities apprehend them. Just as important for Tony, it might prove to be a great story for Tony's next book. But the most important reason for going was that someone in Italy had to answer for the near death of Pauline, Tony's reason for living.

*****

Alitalia Airlines provided plenty of Italian movies with subtitles, so Tony could brush up on his Italian. By the time the plane landed in Rome, he had added these important phrases to his already sparse vocabulary: *Davanti alla porta della latrina, ho mangiato una pizza*—translation, In front of the toilet door, I ate a pizza; and *Il vino di Mario e migliore un cavallo morto*—translation, Mario's wine tastes better than a dead horse.

He found his way to the car rental desk.

"*Voglio affittareuna macchina?*" he asked in his best Italian accent.

"*Tutto ciò che rimane,*" the skinny, young male car rental clerk said and showed him a picture of a tiny two-door Smart Car.

"Shit," said Tony. He signed the papers, grabbed the key fob, took his six-foot frame to the car lot and searched for his five-foot car. His body seemed to know how to contort itself into the tight-fitting interior, and with the help of the GPS, he drove to his hotel, Nazionale 51, across the street from the hotel Laura had booked until Sunday morning.

It was Thursday night, and Tony was beat. Using field glasses, he would have all Friday and Saturday to stake out Laura's hotel entrance through his window overlooking the street. He sacked out on his double-bed, and the busy Roman street noise, two stories below, whispered through his closed window.

He woke up about 5:30 a.m., showered, shaved, dressed and went down to the street. Tony loved European city streets at this time of day. The morning sunrays peeked between buildings and began illuminating the still dark and quiet streets. Small trucks delivered fresh produce, meats, fish and bread to the markets and bakeries.

He crossed the street and followed the scents of espresso and fresh, warm pastries to a bakery that had just opened. Knowing that he might be cooped up in his room all day staking out Laura's hotel, he sat at a sidewalk table with a cappuccino and assorted biscotti and watched Rome awaken in the cool, damp morning summer air. Before leaving, he stocked up at the bakery with several fresh panini, a bottle of mineral water and a six-pack of Moretti beer.

What the hell, he thought. They're probably still asleep. Not much chance of them spotting me. He walked to the main entrance of Eurostars International Palace Hotel and scouted. It was a definitive five-star hotel—a white, five-story, half-block old building with ornate sculptures and a balcony with international flags hanging over the arched entrance, the only way to enter and leave the hotel except for a fire door and loading dock on the side of the structure.

He stood at the entrance and looked up toward the narrow balcony/window of his hotel room. Unless they wore caps, he could spot Laura and Rebecca with ease, run down the staircase from his second-story room and follow them.

Tony had watched enough cop movies and TV shows to enjoy setting up his little espionage station on his tiny balcony complete with a comfortable cushioned chair, binoculars, a bag of sandwiches (panini), ice bucket with a bottle of water in it, a six-pack of beer and even an empty plastic liter bottle to pee in if he didn't want to leave his post.

As Rome got busier and busier, it became more and more difficult to track people leaving and entering the hotel, but Tony kept up with the traffic. Several times he thought he may have spotted Laura and/or Rebecca exiting, but after zooming in tighter or racing down to the street, discovered it wasn't either of them.

Dawn had turned to dusk. After several panini, three cans of beer and a liter bottle full of urine, Tony had had enough. *Maybe I missed them when I followed a false lead on the street or just lost them in a crowd of passersby.* He had to at least find out if they were still registered at the Eurostars Hotel. He abandoned his position, put on a baseball cap and tinted glasses, and headed across the street to the hotel.

Tony felt like the Scarecrow entering the Wizard of Oz's palace when he stepped into the lobby. Smooth brown marble pillars on white-washed pedestals supported the tall arched sculptured ceiling. The two rows of pillars that stood on the mirror-clean brown and white marble floor formed a long runway lit by chandeliers that ended at a long dark-wood reception desk.

As Tony approached the desk clerk, who was dressed in an emblem-blazer and red tie, he almost expected him to say, "The Wizard will not see you today. Come back tomorrow." Instead the smiling young man said, *"Buongiorno."*

Tony knew that most every hotel receptionist in Rome knew English, but when in a foreign country it's always more polite to struggle with the home language. "*Buongiorno, mi scusi,* but uh Laura DiFoggio and her daughter are guests here. I was supposed to meet them in the lobby. Could you please *telefonare* their *camera, per favore?*"

"Of course," he said with an accent but perfect enunciation. "What is the room number, sir?"

"Oh, I can't remember, *mi dispiace.*"

"No, problem. DiFoggio?" the clerk asked, but it must have been a rhetorical question because he typed the name into his computer and didn't look toward Tony for a response. "Now it is my turn to say, 'I'm sorry.' The lady and her daughter checked out yesterday morning."

"Shit!" said Tony and slapped his palm on the desk.

PIER

Tony glanced at the address on the birthday card envelope on the passenger seat of his Smart car:
Pier Sagona
113 Via Ceccano
Frosinone, Italia 03100
"Merge right onto A1/E45 Toll Road," said the GPS lady voice, and Tony left the outskirts of Rome. It was early Saturday morning. After hearing the disappointing news that Laura and Rebecca had checked out on Thursday and he had wasted Friday playing stake-out-cop, Tony treated himself to a hearty Italian dinner at an upscale restaurant and too many *limoncellos* afterward. Much to his amazement, instead of awakening to a hangover, his brain yielded an idea; if he couldn't find Laura, maybe he could find Todd. It was obvious Todd's biological mother wanted Todd to find her by leaving a birthday card trail of envelopes over the years with her return address on them. Having a secret mom living in a little European village might have provided a perfect hideaway for a guy running from the mob in America. Even if Todd wasn't there, his mother might lead Tony to him . . . and Laura.

If Pier Sagona, Todd's real mother, couldn't help him, Tony had nowhere to go but back to the U.S.A.

He felt relieved as he revved the engine of his little Smart car and merged onto the toll road. *Autostratas*, as they're called in Italy, offer easier driving conditions for Americans than the narrow one-way streets within the large Italian cities. "Italians drive like maniacs," returning American tourists had warned Tony before his first trip to Italy several years prior; however, Tony developed a different theory.

His words: "Italians don't know how to drive. Somehow they must just sign up and get a license. Sign again and buy a car. Skim the owner's manual and then hit the road. That's it. Sure, Italy has driving laws, but everyone pretty much ignores them. Once Italian motorists beeped and hailed Italian obscenities at me in Rome because I ignorantly waited for a red stoplight to turn green at a busy intersection instead of shooting through when traffic cleared.

And parking? They can't park. If they see a space, they aim the front end at it and leave it. Cars protrude at all angles from the curb. I think Germans specifically developed the Smart car for Italian drivers; there's no ass end to stick out into traffic when it's parked. When Pauline and I were in Florence, I parallel parked a rented SUV on a busy street. When we got out, a small group of observers had formed. '*Comehai fatto?*' meaning, 'How you do that?' an elderly man asked. They marveled at me like I was a magician."

After about an hour of *autostrata* driving, the GPS voice ordered him onto an off-ramp and toward the village of Frosinone. As he left the ramp and drove onto a two-lane road, he glanced into his rearview mirror. A dark blue sedan parked halfway down the ramp began to move as if the driver was waiting to see which way Tony turned.

Am I being followed? The GPS directed him into several nameless streets, through the quiet village and onto a winding residential road named Via Ceccano. About an acre of hilly, green landscape separated the homes. Gravel driveways led to either ranch or two-story stucco houses with terra cotta roofs set back in rural settings. Tony couldn't see any vehicles in his mirrors and credited his notion of being followed to his imagination. Via Ceccano dead-ended, and the GPS voice announced, "You have reached your destination."

Tony cut the soft, percolating engine of the Smart car at the foot of the driveway. He just sat as if in a trance for a few minutes until he heard himself say aloud, "Beautiful. I could live here."

The gravel-and-sand driveway curved upward onto a knoll and ended at the two-story red clay dwelling. A flat-stone terrace spread like an apron into a semicircle from the main entrance to the ends of the house. A thick, double-trunk tree grew from the middle of the terrace and twisted upward, stretching its strong, leafy branches outward and providing natural shade over the house and terrace. A knee-high round stone wall surrounded the trunk as if the tree sprouted from a deep well, and bright yellow and red flowers sprang from the black dirt that filled the well to the top. The same type of stone wall trimmed the terrace perimeter and another formed a border behind the house that framed a mountain view in the distance. Where the driveway met the house, an outdoor stairway led to a second dwelling.

On the terrace, a senior, thin woman wearing a long black dress and thick gray/black hair combed into a tight bun rocked in a wicker rocker near a matching breakfast table set with three chairs. She appeared oblivious to Tony's presence. He took some pictures with his iPhone camera to capture this mesmerizing view.

As he ascended the hill on foot, a yapping little short-haired dog approached him from beneath the woman's chair. Since the dog wagged its tail and retreated a little with each yap, Tony continued up the hill.

The woman didn't attempt to silence the dog and stiffened into a fearful yet threatening glare as Tony drew nearer.

He smiled and said, "*Buongiorno. Mi scuzi, signora. Mi chiamo Tony Morelli, Americano. Mi Italiano . . .* not so good."

Possibly amused at Tony's vulnerability, she smiled and said, "*Mi Inglese* not so good." In a hoarse but loud voice, she turned toward the top of the stairs and said, "Gina! Gina, *Vieni qui!*"

Almost like magic, a woman appeared at the top of the stairs, on the balcony of the upstairs dwelling. She wore a short flowered summer dress and flip-flops. She pinned her shoulder length dark brown hair behind her head as she skipped down the stairs and approached them.

The older woman spoke several sentences to her. She nodded but kept her eyes on Tony until the woman finished.

"My name is Gina, and this is my Aunt Pier," she said in perfect English with only a slight Italian accent. "She tells me you are American and speak very little Italian. How can we help you?"

Something about her reminded Tony of Pauline. Maybe it was her undetermined age. Her natural beauty, slight figure and perpetual smile made her look Tony's age or even decades younger. Maybe it was the way wisps of her hair dangled in front of her ears whenever she wore her hair up which made a woman look strangely seductive to Tony. Her wide grin exposed perfect white teeth and identical dimples on each cheek. *Any man could easily fall in love with this woman.*

"Yes, my name is Tony Morelli. I'm a writer from Chicago. I don't know how familiar you are with this situation, but I believe a childhood friend of mine who grew up in the United States is also, was also, your aunt's son."

He handed the family picture from Laura's mantel to Gina. She glanced at it without any expression and passed it to her Aunt.

Pier's face softened into a warm smile. *"Sì, Teodoro, mio figlio,"* she said. *"Come lo conoscevi?"*

"Yes, that is her son," Gina translated. "She wants to know how you knew him."

Tony was on the spot. How much should he tell her? There was so much to say, but he didn't want to overload her with information: his alleged encounter with Todd or Teodoro in Palermo after the suicide, the money skimming scandal, the mob, the car bombing and Laura's flight. She was his final lead, and he didn't want to scare her away.

Rather than lie, he decided to just tell the simple truth; he wanted to learn as much about his former friend as he could for a possible short story, essay or book. He could ask about the more sinister aspects later, as necessary, so he shared with Gina his childhood memories of Todd. She translated them to Pier who listened like a child hearing a pleasant fairytale.

"I only know a little about Todd's coming to America," he said. "His adopting father was a chaplain in the U.S. military. He met you when you were in a hospital being treated for injuries when your village was burned. I was sorry to hear that Todd's real father was killed in that bombing."

As Gina translated, Pier's face tightened into a quizzical, confused expression. Her face froze in that look. She shook her head, held the photo in front of Tony and pointed to Reverend David Kenilworth.

"*Questo è il suovero padre.*"

"This is his real father," said Gina.

"Do you mind if I sit down?" asked Tony.

Gina pulled out a chair from the table, and Tony sat.

He was in for more surprises.

GINA

"Chiedeteglise vuoleuna bevanda."

"My aunt wants to know if you would like something to drink," Gina said to Tony.

"Only if you two ladies will join me."

Gina translated and moved toward the stairs, but Pier said something to her that sounded like "Sit down" and Gina sat at the table with Tony. Pier disappeared inside her first floor dwelling.

"You seemed surprised at what my aunt said about the father," said Gina.

"Yes, I was led to believe that your aunt . . . ," Tony paused. Was it necessary to say that his story was that her aunt was a pregnant prostitute and the father died in a false flag bombing?

"I'm afraid I cannot help you fill in the blanks, Mr. Morelli—"

"Tony. You can call me Tony."

"Tony, you see, I've only been living with my aunt for the past few months."

Tony followed her gaze over the low stone wall and into the distance at the blue mountain range. *Maybe she's thinking about her past. Maybe she's wondering if she should share her family secrets with this stranger.*

After a short silence, she said, "My grandfather built this house himself."

"It's a beautiful place."

"Yes, my father, aunt and grandparents lived here. They rented the upstairs to tourists and ran a restaurant in town. They all worked in that restaurant, but my father never liked working in the family business. When he grew up he moved to Siracusa, Sicily and bought an *agriturismo*."

"I'm sorry. What is an *agri*–?" Tony stumbled at the pronunciation.

"—*turismo*," she said and smiled like a teacher helping a struggling student. "That is a small farm, but also more. If the owner rents some living quarters out for tourism, the Italian government allows for a tax grant. It is a way to encourage tourism."

"Sounds smart."

"Yes, my father was a smart man. It is the only thing he had in common with his father. They, my father and grandfather, did not get along. They did not speak to each other for many years. That is why we knew nothing of what went on here for a long time, including my aunt and her children."

"Children?"

"Gina, *Vieni qui. Ho bisogno di te.*" Pier's voice resonated from inside the house.

"Excuse me," said Gina. "My aunt needs me." She hustled toward the patio door.

Tony sat back and exposed his face to the sun outside of the tree shade. It was a comfortable warmth, not sticky or tepid, just cozy and enlightening.

Gina appeared carrying a tray holding three water glasses, three wine glasses and a clear glass bowl full of ice. Pier followed with an opened bottle of red wine and a liter bottle of mineral water. They set the tray and bottles onto the table. Pier said, "*Mi, scuzi,*" and went back into the house.

Gina gave her a querulous look, turned back toward Tony, smiled and filled the water glasses with ice. "My aunt says that in the summer you must cool the skin with cold water and warm the heart with red wine. This is called Nero D'Avola, a staple wine of southern Italy and Sicily. Most Americans think only of chianti in straw baskets when they think of Italian wine."

Tony knew of Nero D'Avola but kept quiet. He let Gina pour the wine and provide information at will. "So, Gina, what about you? What brings you here, away from your roots in Sicily?"

She sat and sipped from her water glass.

"Well, I grew up on the *agriturismo* and went to school in Siracusa. Later, I went to the University of Palermo and studied international economics. After graduation, I worked at a large bank in Siracusa. That is where I met my fiancé, Tommaso. He is a bank administrator. How about you, Tony? Are you married?"

"No, I'm afraid I'm not very good at marriage. I'm divorced, but I have a girlfriend who I met on a trip here to Italy."

"Really? Is she Italian?"

"No, we were both Americans on a tour escaping bad relationships in the states."

"And you fell in love in Italy. How romantic."

"Yes, I guess so. Don't you miss your fiancé in Sicily?"

"Oh, no. He now works at Banca D'Italia in Rome."

"That's on Via Nazionale, just down the street from my hotel."

"Yes, and as you know by now, only about an hour or so from here. My aunt and I reconnected when I sent out announcements of my engagement less than a year ago. She invited me here to visit, but work in Siracusa kept me away. Last winter, she asked me to come and to meet her son who was visiting with his sister from the U.S. That was your friend, Teodoro, or as you called him, Todd."

Tony nodded.

"But I never got the chance. Before I could get away for a visit, his tragic death happened in Rome. His sister insisted the body be sent home immediately for the funeral and burial, but my aunt arranged for a memorial mass at her church here in town. I came and stayed for a few days to comfort her.

"When I told her about Tommaso's transfer to the Bank in Rome, she asked me to come live in her upstairs apartment. It seemed like a perfect arrangement, so I quit my job in Siracusa and came to live here. During the week, I stay here with her. On weekends, either Tommaso comes here or I stay with him in the city."

"So, when is the big wedding day?"

"In October. I'd like to live here, but Tommaso wants to live in Rome. We're still undecided."

The patio screen door slid open and Pier came out carrying what looked like one of those miniature Italian accordions. It was actually a photo album. The laminated pages seemed to struggle to push against the covers and to reveal its pictures. Pier let the pages fan open as she plopped the album onto the table.

Tony and Gina, like children preparing to hear their mother read to them, moved their chairs closer toward Pier. Pier smiled and started with the first page of photographs. Tony felt she respected his limited Italian vocabulary and kept her explanations brief. "*Mi nonna e nonno,*" she said and pointed to yellowed tintype photos of her grandparents.

With every sip of Nero D'Avola and every page turn, Tony felt a warmth toward Gina and Pier. The chronology of photos revealed Pier emerging from a beautiful, happy child into a striking, voluptuous young woman.

Tony put his hand on a page as soon as he saw it—a blurry snapshot taken of a woman sitting up in a hospital bed. Her face looked drawn, smiling but also a little sad. She held what looked like two loosely wrapped bread loaves in front of her.

He pointed to the snapshot and asked, "*Capisco?*"

"*Sono ioei mieifigli gemelli,*" said Pier, "*Teodoro e Vincenzo.*"

"She said, 'It is I and my twin sons, Teodoro and Vincenzo,'" Gina translated.

Pier put her hands over her face and wept.

VINCENZO

Tony maneuvered his Smart cart as if it were a lab rat going through a maze. He wanted to get out of Frosinone as soon as possible and onto the *autostrata*. The ease of driving on a four-lane highway without stops and heavy traffic allowed him to think. He needed to make sense of all he had just learned from Aunt Pier and what he had volunteered to do for her.

*****

"Excuse us for a moment, Tony," said Gina. "I need to talk with my aunt."

"Of course."

He took his glass of wine and walked to the low stone wall that ran behind the house. If Gina meant that Tony should get into his car and go, he wasn't leaving—not after hearing that Todd had a twin.

The blue mountains in the distance still looked hazy from the morning cloud cover. Between the wall and the mountain range, a valley of green hills sloped downwards toward the base of the mountains where the bright red roofs of another little village reflected the morning sun.

Strange, the mountains are foggy, but the village is clear—like what I just learned about Todd; he had or has a twin. Where is this Vincenzo? Is he alive? If so, is this the person I saw in Palermo?

At first, Gina and Pier talked in hushed voices even though Tony wouldn't have understood much of their Italian conversation anyway. The voices grew louder. At times it even sounded like angry shouting, but sometimes that's just the demonstrative nature of Italian communication. After a long silence, Tony returned to the table and sat.

"I'll be leaving in a minute. I'm sorry, and I don't wish to pry into very private matters, but this news about the twin brother—"

"It was news to me, too, Tony. I apologize for asking you to leave, but I needed answers. Even though my father's side of the family was . . . what's the word in English?"

"Estranged?"

"Yes, I still wanted to know why she kept it a secret so long that I had another cousin."

"Gina, I didn't tell you this because I didn't think it was important. I was here in Italy not long ago on a book tour. I thought for sure that I had encountered Todd, but I later found out that Todd had already died. That's what inspired me to research his life for a book. Is it possible that I actually saw Vincenzo?"

Gina looked at Tony as if he had two heads. "After what my aunt just told me, yes, it is possible."

"As I said before, I don't wish to pry, but can you share with me what she told you? It's important to my research about Todd, but maybe there's some way I can help you and your aunt, too."

Gina spoke several sentences in Italian to Pier. When she finished, the old woman just nodded and looked into her lap.

"I told my aunt that we've had far too many secrets in this family, and that maybe you could help us in some way. She agrees."

Tony nodded, and Gina continued.

"My aunt was only sixteen when she met the American military man, a chaplain, at the family restaurant. They, at least she, fell in love. She hid her pregnancy from the family as long as she could. You must understand that an unwed mother, especially a very young one, was a disgrace to a Catholic family back then.

"My uncle sent her to relatives in Tivoli, near Rome. He told her not to return with a bastard baby. When the twins were born, the father, the military chaplain, took one child back to the United States. The other they left at the altar of the Roman Catholic Diocese of Tivoli Church."

"And what became of him?" asked Tony.

"*Dove si trovaora Vincenzo?*" Gina asked Pier.

Tony expected a short, definitive response, but Pier broke into a lengthy monologue. It ended with her speaking as if she were in church and looking off into the distance.

Gina hesitated before speaking. It would have been difficult for anyone to translate every word, verbatim, of Pier's speech.

"My aunt said that her father forbid her to find out. She went back to the church a year later anyway, but they would not tell her anything except that he is in 'God's hands.' She tried to write to the father, but he never responded to her letters. Still, she sent Teodoro a birthday card every year."

Tony remembered the wood-carved box and nodded.

"But here's the interesting part," said Gina. "My aunt told this same story to Teodoro and his sister when they came for a visit last winter. The next day they left. They said that they wanted to tour more of Italy and then return to the States. Within a few weeks, she read about Teodoro's suicide in Rome."

"Tell your aunt that I'll find Vincenzo."

Tony heard himself say these words as if someone else had made him say them.

*****

Tell your aunt that I'll find Vincenzo!" he said in a comic-book-heroic voice that made him laugh as he turned off the *autostrata* and drove toward his hotel in downtown Rome. *What the hell was I thinking when I said that? I'm Superman? Mighty Mouse? The answer was not as amusing to him: I was thinking that a search for Vincenzo might lead to Todd, or Teodoro and Laura.*

He looked for a parking space near his hotel, saw a tiny spot a half block away, and turned into it *because, a Smart car can find space almost anywhere.*

TRUE CONFESSIONS

Tony gathered his paraphernalia from the passenger seat and crammed it inside his manila folder. The stuff included the Kenilworth family picture, his notes, and a card Gina had given him with her fiancé's work phone, his Rome address and her cell phone number. Before entering his hotel, he again got the feeling that he was being followed. He turned and looked at the entrance of the Eurostars Palace Hotel across the street. A medium built, tall bald guy dressed in a brown suit stared at him. Tony pretended to enter his hotel, but turned back as if the man had called him in an effort to catch the guy watching him.

The bald man was gone.

The red message light on his room blinked, and Tony hit the play button. "Hey, baby, it's your red-headed singer. Hope you got there and everything's okay. It's about eight in the morning here in Chi-town, or should I say at our Oak Park apartment? I'm leaving to rehearse with the band. I think my pipes still work, but I'll let the guys judge, especially when I sing the last note of 'Blue Bayou.' Call me tonight. Love ya."

Tony treated himself to dinner and wine at a plush restaurant, Aroma. It offered a stellar night view of the Colosseum. He sensed the irony of this magnificent sight with every sip of Nero D'Avola wine. Tourists and locals marvel at this iconic arena. Their eyes let them see it, but their ears don't let them hear the screams of the Christians being torn apart and eaten by lions. It reminded him that he had to visit a church in Tivoli the next morning.

He set his alarm for three a.m. so he could call Pauline at a reasonable Chicago time. For some reason he had a recurring dream during this trip. He imagined he was a character in the movie *All the Presidents' Men*, the film about The Washington Post reporters Bernstein and Woodward uncovering the Watergate scandal that led to Nixon's resignation. Sometimes he was Dustin Hoffman (Bernstein). Sometimes he was Robert Redford (Woodward). This time, Jason Robards (executive editor Ben Bradlee) was berating Tony, who seemed to be both Bernstein and Woodward when his alarm went off.

*****

Tony expected to hear a standard "Hello" when Pauline answered. Instead, she just said, "Come home."

"Why? What's going on back there?"

"Nothing. I just miss you?"

"I miss you, too, but remember? You told me to 'Go to Italy, and get that bitch.'"

"I know, but I was pissed off. Now, I want you back. Did you find her?"

"Not yet, but I'm on to something."

"Oh, by the way, three cops came looking for you a couple hours after your plane took off."

"Three?"

He had figured Bianco and Kaminski might have wanted to talk to him. But who was the third person? "What did they want?"

"They wouldn't say. They just seemed concerned when I told them you had left for Rome."

Tony filled her in on his trip to Pier's house and all he had learned. He left out his suspicions about being followed—no need to worry her. "Just make sure that if you find her, you don't try to be a hero," Pauline said. "Notify the police, here and there, and let them take care of it."

"Okay, Mom."

"I'm serious, Tony. I know you. Whenever you smell a good story, especially one with some mystery, you get obsessive and the next thing you know you're in danger."

A silence followed as Tony recalled his last book about an actor that drew him to Hollywood where he had got beaten up, jailed and damn near killed. It was time to change the subject.

"So, you said you went to a rehearsal. How's the voice?"

"Smoky. Seriously. Remember when that music reviewer described my voice that way a few years ago? Well, that's what the boys in the band call me now. No, the voice is fine. As a matter of fact, I think I expanded my range another octave lower. Maybe I'll blow up another Jeep tomorrow."

Tony laughed and said, "Hey, I'm a little horny. How about some phone sex? What are you wearing?"

"Well, I'm lying on the couch watching TV, and you know that black lace little teddy with the tiny rose near the crotch?"

"Yeah."

"It's in the wash; I'm naked."

After teasing each other, they said their "I-love-yous" and ended the call.

*****

A cobblestone front yard of the Roman Catholic Diocese of Tivoli Church now served as a parking lot for the old cathedral. Tony pulled into the lot off Via Santa Anna and parked in a tiny space between two large cars. He was starting to get used to crunching his tall frame into the Smart car and to enjoy finding parking spots in the smallest of spaces.

Before entering he stood in the lot and admired the front of the church. Three two-story archways with wrought iron decorative gates protected the centuries-old wooden doors. The gates between the center archway opened to the main entrance, huge double doors with Saint Joseph carved on one, and Saint Mary carved on the other—both with open arms and palms.

The interiors of old cathedrals in Europe seemed to share the same purpose—make the entrants feel as if they stepped between heaven and earth. The dark, dank section of pews gave congregations the feeling of being on the cold earth, but the candle lit perimeter and stained-glass windows, in particular the one behind the white floral adorned altar of Christ holding a child, suggested a world bright as heaven beyond.

A sparse group of people sat at random on one side of church. Tony wondered if a mass was scheduled, *but why are they sitting on only side of the church?* Tony joined them in the back pew. The answer came after a few minutes. A boy about thirteen or fourteen years old stepped out of the ominous dark wood confessional box. Two sour-faced parents led him outside the church where Tony was confident the question would be "So what penance did the Father give you for your terrible sin?"

The scene was all too familiar to Tony. He had stopped attending church sometime after or during high school, but he still maintained a nagging faith in a higher being despite his rational belief in science. Nuns, priests and his dad had drilled a real fear of God into him during his pre-adolescent years; it was confession on Saturday and mass on Sunday.

He always remembered his last confession. He had dropped his pencil during math class in the seventh grade. When he reached into the aisle to pick it up, he noticed that Linda Crocetti wasn't wearing underpants. The sight intrigued him: those smooth white thighs, that curious erotic body part, that stinging pain from Sister Margaret's ruler slapped on the back of his neck.

"Anthony, what are you doing?"

"Just picking up my pencil, Sister."

She must have noticed that the pencil wasn't the only straight thing he had gotten from the experience.

"I'm calling your parents to make sure you go to confession this Saturday."

While Tony reminisced, people entered and left the confessional box until only an elderly couple dressed in black remained in the congregation. The confession box door opened, and a woman left the church.

The old couple motioned for Tony to go ahead of them. Tony tried to mime that he wasn't there for confession, but the two people continued to coax him. Tony looked like he was playing Charades and doing a lousy job when the priest's door of the confessional box opened and a heavyset priest with thick dark hair and black-rimmed glasses stepped out. The old man and woman spoke to him in Italian. The priest motioned for Tony to enter the box, said, "*Andiamo*" and reentered the box.

Tony felt like that God-fearing kid he used to be as he walked toward the gloomy brown wooden confessional box. He remembered how, as a kid, it reminded him of an old-fashioned telephone booth where the priest sat and a connected smaller phoning stall for sinners. The darkness inside intensified his latent fear. The small sliding window between the booths opened, and Tony began speaking as soon as he saw the shadowy face of the priest behind the screen.

"*Mi scusi, Padre. Mi Italiano* not so good, but—"

"No problem, my son," the priest said with a thick Italian accent. "I speak English and several other languages."

"Oh, good. You see—"

"When was your last confession?"

"Uh . . . well, I guess it was when I was twelve or thirteen. See, I dropped my pencil, and the girl behind me wasn't wearing underwear—"

"Stop. Stop. Let's start over. The Catholic ritual for confessions hasn't changed, and it is universal. We'll address your most recent sins. Do you remember how to start?"

Tony felt trapped. He knew he had to play the confession game if he wanted to get information from this priest.

"Bless me, Father, for I have sinned. As I said my last confession was nearly forty years ago. Recently, I've told many lies to get information about a friend who was born here. Now, I've come to find his twin brother who was left on the steps of this very church after birth . . ."

Tony tried to be both thorough and concise as he told the story of Teodoro and Vincenzo. He finished with ". . . and I have come here on behalf of Vincenzo's mother and cousin to locate him."

The priest didn't speak for the greater part of a minute before saying, "Wait for me in the chapel. We'll talk after I hear my last confession."

He stepped outside the box and could tell by the look on the couple's faces that they were sorry that they had let Tony go before them, or maybe it was disdain for this reprobate who had taken so long to confess his lengthy list of sins.

The quiet, peaceful atmosphere within the chapel put Tony into a serene trance while he sat in the pew and waited for the priest.

"The ambiance of God often makes us fall into a tranquil state." The priest's words jolted Tony awake to find the priest sitting next to him. "I apologize for startling you."

"No, no, I'm glad to see you."

"The anonymity respected in confessions left us nameless. I am Father Francesco Pozzo," he said and extended his hand.

"Tony Morelli," he returned and shook the priest's hand. Tony marveled at how he and the priest resembled each other except for an age difference. Father Pozzo seemed a decade younger and much shorter. His demeanor and tone of voice complemented the peaceful nature of the chapel.

"You told an intriguing story. I must tell you that I believe I heard the very same story less than a year ago."

"I'm not surprised. Vincenzo's twin, Teodoro, came from America looking for him last winter."

"Yes, and I believe his sister accompanied him; however, that leaves me with a problem, Mr. Morelli. You see, the church does not give out such private information out so freely. I was reluctant to divulge such information even to his brother and sister, and you are not even related."

Tony anticipated this problem.

"I understand, Father, but there are some circumstances that you must know. Not long after Teodoro and Laura came to you searching for their brother, Teodoro jumped from Victor Emmanuel Monument in Rome to his death."

Father Pozzo closed his eyes and sighed. It was obvious that even if he had learned about the death from the media or some other source, he hadn't associated it with the people he had encountered months ago.

"As I told you in confession, I am here on behalf of the mother who may or may not have one remaining son and needs some closure before her death."

The priest stared at a statue of the Madonna near the altar. He closed his eyes again and mumbled a few words of prayer, opened them and said, "You mentioned something the church told his mother years ago when she left the child."

"They told her that her son was in 'God's hands' now."

"Wait here," said Father Pozzo, and he disappeared through a door behind a tall podium at the front of the chapel.

Tony waited for near half an hour. He thought that the priest had abandoned him, an improbable but easy way to avoid helping him, when he heard a door open and close behind the pedestal.

"Take this," Father Pozzo said and handed a brown envelope to Tony. "Its contents may help you. It contains a brochure, a letter from me if you need a reference on your quest and some other paraphernalia that might benefit you."

Tony thanked the priest, who accepted several euros that Tony donated.

Outside in the sunlight, Tony emptied the contents of the envelope onto the hood of his Smart car. It contained the letter handwritten in Italian, some small pins with the Madonna on the buttons, some holy cards and a brochure. The brochure for The Roman Home for Children had translations in German, French and English. Within its mission statement it listed its core values:

Protect the rights of children;

Promote the highest standards of education, care and treatment of children;

Support and preserve the relationship between a child and his/her family and community;

Assist children and families in all efforts that promote a healthy reintegration at the earliest possible time; Exist as a resource for children and families irrespective of race, ethnicity, gender, age, disability, religion or national origin.

Accept all children from THE HANDS OF GOD.

The holy cards featured St. Anthony, the patron saint of lost souls.

Tony gathered the material back into the envelope, put a holy card in his wallet and left in his Smart car.

ORPHANS

Robert Redford stood over Tony as he typed his story in the newsroom of The Washington Post. Jason Robards walked up to both of them and yelled at them in Italian. Tony turned around, and Pauline motioned for him to join her in the elevator. He walked toward the bank of elevators, and a bald guy followed him. By the time he reached the elevator, the doors had closed.

When they reopened, Jason Robards continued yelling at him in Italian. Father Pozzo beckoned him to escape in the stairwell. Tony literally flew down the stairs and knocked down Gina who waited for him at the bottom. He awakened from his latest *All The President's Men* dream and knew exactly what this dream meant.

He retrieved Gina's cell phone number from his notes in the manila folder and called from his hotel room phone.

"*Pronto.*"

"Gina?"

"*Sì.*"

"It's Tony Morelli."

"Tony, how are you?"

"Fine. Listen, you said you'd be willing to help me if I needed it. Well, I think I need it. You see, I've been pretty lucky so far with my shaky command of Italian, but sooner or later I'll need an interpreter. Can you help me? I'll pay you what I can."

"Of course, but you do not have to pay me. Now that I'm not working I have plenty of time, and I am anxious to find my cousin, too."

Tony told her how he had tracked Vincenzo to The Roman Home for Children, and they made plans to meet there in a few hours.

*****

Tony wasn't sure what he expected to see when he parked in front of The Roman Home for Children, but it wasn't this. Maybe he expected a campus of dormitories, a school building and a chapel all built on rolling hills with a playground and sports field in the middle with Father Flanagan hitting fly balls to boys dressed in Boys' Town uniforms. He sat in his Smart car, parked in front of a brick office building, on a busy street in the modern business district of Rome and watched the traffic blur by.

A Vespa motorbike slowed as the driver peered into Tony's window. The driver maneuvered the Vespa, front wheel touching the curb, in the sliver of an opening between Tony's front bumper and another car. Dressed in Nikes, blue jeans, a loose-fitting red windbreaker and a helmet, the short person dismounted the motorbike and approached Tony. If it wasn't for the shortness, Tony would have bet it was the bald guy he thought was following him, but when the helmet came off, it was Gina.

Tony rolled down the window and said, "Are you the Italian version of The Hell's Angels?"

"Sorry?"

"Never mind it's an American joke."

"If I may borrow your English word and expression, where the hell's the orphanage?"

Tony laughed and stretched his tall body out of the tiny car.

"You must be terribly uncomfortable. I mean being so tall and that tiny auto."

"Actually, I'm starting to get used to it," Tony said and pulled the brochure from his manila folder. They both examined it, and the address was right. The building directory indicated that it was on the second floor; they took the stairs. The stenciled doors indicated that the entire level housed departments of The Roman Home for Children, but there wasn't a kid in sight.

Gina and a smiling young receptionist exchanged *buongiornos,* and Gina asked a simple question. The receptionist returned a long explanation that generated a series of questions from Gina followed by lengthy, patient responses from the receptionist.

Gina excused herself from her conversation, and turned toward Tony.

"It seems we are a decade or so late for orphanages in Italy."

Tony looked confused.

"There are still some orphanages scattered throughout Italy, but most are state run institutions or centers for placing children in what you call in America foster homes. At one time, in particular after World War II, there were many orphanages. The Catholic Church ran most of them. Overcrowding and underfunding led to their eventual downfall. The government took over and established this program. Homeless children are brought here, and directed to foster care or state run children's facilities."

"So, this is kind of like a clearinghouse for kids. Great, but that doesn't help us."

"Maybe it will. It also houses the files from all the orphanages that existed in Italy since World War II, assuming of course that orphanages or their records were not destroyed in the war."

"Well, let's end the suspense. Ask her about Vincenzo."

"*Avete leregistrazioni di,*" Gina paused and then said the name as if she were speaking to a six-year old, "Vincenzo Sagona?"

The receptionist typed into her computer. Within seconds, she turned toward Tony and Gina and said, "Si."

The two acted like children who had just entered an amusement park, but their joy was short-lived. After Gina asked if they could see the file, the young receptionist said with the same painted-on smile, "No."

The amusement park was closed. In further conversation with the receptionist, Gina learned that the computer's basic information revealed that Vincenzo had grown up in an orphanage that the Roman Catholic Church operated. Only the church, not even family members, could authorize release of the files.

Tony produced the letter Father Pozzo had written for him. The receptionist read the letter and her smile disintegrated. Tony had gotten the impression that up to this point their inquiry was routine for the receptionist. A typical end of these encounters was disappointed relatives leaving and this greeter returning to her comfort zone. Now she had to leave her station and search through files in some musty record room.

As soon as she left the reception area, Tony and Gina acted like school kids taking a test while the teacher left the room. He turned the computer screen toward them and gave Gina his notepad and pen to take notes.

Hearing high heels clicking in the hallway toward them, Gina scribbled her final notes. Tony flicked the screen to its original position just as the receptionist, smiling, returned.

"Mi dispiace, il file è mancante."

"Cosa?" asked Gina

"Qualcuno deve averrubatoil contenuto."

"What's the problem?" asked Tony.

"She said the contents of the file must have been stolen."

"What? Are you shittin me?" Tony said to the smiling woman who just looked at him as if he were a whining child. "Go back and look again!"

"Forget it, Tony. She doesn't understand you, and she probably doesn't care," Gina said to him and led him out of the room by his arm. "Anyway, I think I got what we need from the computer."

As they left, Gina mirrored the receptionist's fake smile, said "Ciao" to her and slammed the door.

ESPRESSO AND INSIGHT

Neither Tony nor Gina spoke until they reached the café down the block, where they sat at an outdoor table and each ordered an espresso.

"Well, don't leave me in suspense. What did you find out?" asked Tony.

Gina pulled Tony's notepad from her leather purse and squinted at her writing. "I had to hurry, so my writing is hard to read. The first part was just technical information: his name, date of birth, date admitted to the orphanage and some priest's and nun's signatures. The interesting part came in the medical history."

"Go on."

"His initial examination when he was admitted at two weeks old reported that he was in excellent health. His next examination when he was five indicated . . ." She paused and looked closer at her writing. *"Zoppo elievementeri tardato."*

"Translation?"

"Lame or limping and mildly retarded."

Tony blanched. The limping, disheveled guy he thought was Todd in Palermo—the guy he chased, and who clipped him on the jaw. Could that have been Vincenzo?

Gina continued to scan her notes for significant information. After about a half minute, she shook her head and said, "My notes are hard to read. I scribbled: eight-years old, adopted, Manicomio Provinciale Santa Maria della Pietà."

"So, he was adopted by someone?"

"No, Santa Maria della Pietà was a mental hospital."

"My God, that poor kid," said Tony. He remembered a feature story he had done for an American magazine years ago when he was a reporter, fresh out of college. He researched mental institutions in the States that existed through the 50s and 60s. Prisons treated inmates better than most of these "hell holes," as they were called, treated their patients. Many of these underfunded "hospitals" had patients living together in unsanitary dorms and dungeons.

Patients often suffered from physical and sexual abuse from other patients and sometimes staff. They became victims of cruel treatments and experiments including shock treatment and lobotomies. Although his research focused on American mental institutions, he remembered learning that, in general, European mental facilities were no better and often worse. "Well, I suppose we'll have to prepare for another confrontation with institutional bureaucracy."

"Not this time. Santa Maria della Pietà closed fifteen maybe twenty years ago."

"So, what happened to the patients?"

"I really don't know. You'll have to do some research."

Tony sat back hard in his metal chair and watched pedestrians pass on the square. For the first time since he had landed in Italy, he felt like a complete foreigner, lost and out of place. He wished he were back in Chicago or, to be specific, back in his Oak Park apartment and snuggling with Pauline.

"Hey, Tony, you look, as I have heard Americans say, out-of-it."

"Oh sorry, Gina. Just all of sudden I felt a little homesick."

"Very understandable. Listen, I'll be staying here in Rome for a few days with Tommaso, my fiancé. Why don't you join us for dinner tomorrow evening?"

"No, no, I don't want to intrude."

"Nonsense, Tommaso would like to meet you, and I won't take no for an answer."

She scribbled something on a napkin and gave it to Tony.

"Here show this to the padrone, the hotel manager. He'll tell you how to get there. I'll make a reservation for seven p.m." She gave him a peck on the cheek, and he returned one—the European sign of friendship; she left.

*****

Nazionale 51, Tony's hotel, provided modest accommodations compared to the Eurostars International Palace Hotel where Laura and Rebecca had stayed, but it served his needs well, including a clean small room and free Wi-Fi. Tony had all the most recent computer gadgets, but he preferred traveling with his old laptop; its big screen and full size keyboard reminded him that he was a serious writer and not some kid on the subway with a smart phone texting gossip to his peers.

At the small desk at the end of his single bed he Googled Manicomio Provinciale Santa Maria della Pietà and found this article:

The old "Manicomio Provinciale Santa Maria della Pietà" had been the main psychiatric hospital in Rome (Piazza S. Maria della Pietà, 5) until its closure in 1999. The first stone of the buildings was placed - in the presence of the King Vittorio Emanuele III on the 28th of June 1909 and the construction was finished after less than two years, on the 31th of May 1911.

The new "Manicomio Provinciale" took the name of Santa Maria della Pietà only in 1926, when the ancient psychiatric hospital on Lungara Street was finally closed. The "Manicomio Provinciale" was immersed in a park and consisted of 43 buildings, 29 of them dedicated to the wards. Nowadays, some pavilions have been restored and dedicated to various health-care services, while many others still remain abandoned.

Pavilion 6 hosts the Museo Laboratorio della Mente, a museum devoted to the history of psychiatry. The first Director of the hospital, from 1913 to 1938, was Augusto Giannelli; under him the structure, originally designed to host 1000 mentally ill, reached the figure of 2602.

Tony stepped onto his narrow balcony that overlooked Via Nazionale. Near the Eurostars International Palace Hotel entrance a disheveled man wearing worn, dirty clothing with his pant leg rolled up exposing a stub sat on the sidewalk with an emaciated dog sleeping next to him.

"If that mental hospital closed down in 1999, what the hell happened to 2602 patients?" Tony said aloud as if someone stood next to him.

A man dropped some euros into the amputee's lap and entered the lush hotel. It was the bald guy Tony had thought was following him.

DOVE VECCHIO GIUSEPPE?

Tony woke up early the next morning from a dreamless sleep. He was glad. That chronic *All The President's Men* dream frustrated him. The dream meant that his subconscious was trying to tell him something, and interpreting both a foreign language and his own vague thoughts gave him headaches.

An idea greeted him that morning. The answer to his question, what the hell happened to 2602 mental patients, or to be more specific what the hell happened to Vincenzo Sagona, might lie at the Rome law enforcement agency. In Chicago, his cop friends proved to be good resources for Chicago history, so maybe it was true in Rome, also.

His day started with a simple question for the hotel desk clerk, "Where is the closest police station?"

"That depends. Do you want the *Polizia di Stato, the Carabinieri* or the *Polizia Municipale?*"

"I don't know. What's the difference?"

"Let me ask you, signore, what is it you need?"

"I need to know what happened to a certain mental patient when the mental hospital here in Rome closed."

"Probably the *Polizia Municipale* would be of assistance. The main headquarters is about five minutes away on Via della Greca."

He gave Tony directions, and Tony thanked him; however, before leaving he asked, "Just out of curiosity, if there were a robbery, murder or even a suicide, which agency would show up?"

The clerk answered as if it were a common question. "Probably all of them. They would spend a few minutes arguing over jurisdiction before anything got done."

*****

The police headquarters looked like something from an old movie set in the precinct of a rough neighborhood in the Bronx or the south side of Chicago. The old four story red brick building looked battered and tired. All the third and fourth floor windows were closed and barred. The other windows on the bottom floors stood wide open. The heat on the street poured inside and seemed to force the sounds of whirring fans, clacking keyboards and conversation back onto the pavement.

Tony entered the main double doors without his interpreter, Gina. He'd see her and her fiancé at dinner that night and didn't want to bother her more than he needed; he figured that a police department in such a tourist city as Rome would probably have officers who were multilingual.

"*Mi scusi, parli inglese?*" he asked a young officer dressed in the summer uniform of a short sleeved white shirt and white hat and seated behind the front desk.

"Yes, what can I do for you?"

"I'm looking for a friend who once resided at the mental institution, Manicomio Provinciale, and disappeared when it closed in, I believe, 1999."

The young officer nodded, picked up the desk phone, and spoke a few sentences before directing Tony to a second floor office.

"*Buongiorno,*" said a middle-aged officer dressed like the front desk officer but more casual with his shirt unbuttoned at the top and no hat. He sat behind a wooden desk in a small office with file cabinets, books and many family pictures set on top of nearly every feasible place. "The desk sergeant tells me you are American and looking for someone. My name is Tenente, Lieutenant, Carboni."

Tony introduced himself and related his whole story starting with his encounter with either Todd or Vincenzo in Palermo. He felt very comfortable talking to this guy who seemed to be a seasoned cop with time on his hands.

Carboni nodded with a concerned look on his face as Tony spoke. When he finished, the officer stopped nodding but stared into space with the same intense expression. He swiveled his chair to face his computer and said, "What was his name again, and when did he disappear?"

"Vincenzo Sagona, sometime around or after 1999."

Carboni typed onto his keyboard and within seconds a photo popped onto the screen. He turned the monitor in Tony's view and said, "Is that the man?"

Except for the longer disheveled hair and a younger face, it was a ringer for the guy who knocked out Tony in Palermo.

"Yes, I believe so."

Carboni turned the screen back into his view, scrolled up and read aloud, "Vincenzo Sagona, arrested twice in the summer of 1999. Small stuff—vagrancy, shoplifting. Not surprising."

"What do you mean?"

He laughed to himself. "I was working the streets back then. In America I think you call them beat cops. What a summer, the summer of '99 in Rome."

Tony looked confused.

Carboni put his hands behind his head and sat back on his chair.

"The government shut down the Manicomio Provinciale, the mental hospital here in Rome."

Tony pretended to hear the name for the first time and appeared intrigued. He wanted to learn all the details, and Carboni seemed to want to share this memorable cop story.

"Yes, it was a bad time to be a *Polizia Municipale*," he said but laughed as he reminisced. "The problem was that the government had no plan of what to do with the *brevetti mentali*."

Tony's puzzled expression prompted Carboni to translate.

"The mental patients. Oh yes, if they could locate family, the officials gave these poor souls to them, but most family had abandoned them, and many families that claimed them did the same thing the government did; they let them loose onto the Roman streets. Most of them did not know how to survive.

"We, the police working the streets, dealt with every kind of petty problem; shoplifting, pickpockets, loitering, harassment, urinating and defecating in public, but mostly their presence. . . How do you say in America? 'Scared the shit' out of citizens," he said, threw his head back and laughed. He straightened up in his chair and grew more serious as he continued.

"The government predicted an even bigger problem. In several months the whole world would be celebrating *Millennio*, The Millenium. Many tourists planned vacations to historic places: Paris, London, Rome. The Rome bureaucrats couldn't risk the threat of losing tourism currency because of the *brevetti mentali*. As most politicians do, they disguised their scheme to look like an act of charity. They planned a pre-holiday dinner for unfortunate vagrants. They had us street police gather them up and load them onto municipal busses and bring them to large meeting halls for a fabulous feast. After the dinner, we loaded them back onto the busses that took them to various cities throughout Italy and left them."

Tony sighed and looked at the floor as he sensed the obvious.

"Yes you see, my friend, your Vincenzo Sagona might be here in Rome or a hundred other places," said Carboni and gazed out his window. "There is one sure way to find him, however, if he is still in Rome."

Tony peered up, and Carboni swiveled from his view of the Roman street, met Tony's stare with a mischievous smile and said, "*Vecchio Giuseppe, Re dei Mendicanti.*"

"Sorry, *non capisco.*"

"Old Giuseppe, King of the Beggars. If anyone would know the whereabouts of this Vincenzo person, it would be him. He is one of our most precious informants."

"So where do I find this Old Giuseppe?"

Carboni's mischievous smile expanded as he pointed out the window and said, "He's somewhere out there. If you want to find him, you must enter their, the beggars', world. You can't enter dressed like you are."

Tony eyed his casual, but clean summer khaki slacks and white short-sleeved Polo shirt.

"You need not dress like another beggar, but if you look too clean and too sophisticated, they will be suspicious of you and not help you. You must, I believe the English expression is 'dress down' to them. You need only this question, '*dove Vecchio Giuseppe?*' meaning 'where is Old Giuseppe?' Say it for me."

"*Dove Vecchio Giuseppe?*" Tony repeated several times to meet Carboni's approval.

"Good, now you need only one more important thing, euros."

"Euros?"

"Yes, these people don't give information for nothing, especially Giuseppe. You will be surprised to find that our beggars are not greedy. They don't require much, but they know how to survive. They are also very grateful. They often reward the smallest token, even just a smile, with '*Dio vi benedica*,' God bless you."

Tony thought about the beggars he had encountered thousands of miles away in both Chicago and New York.

"I guess some things are universal, Tenente Carboni. If I should find this Old Giuseppe, does he understand English? I mean, should I bring an interpreter?"

"Interesting you should mention 'universal things.' *Sciarade*, I believe the English word is Charades, is a universal game. You will need to be good at *Sciarade* if you wish to communicate with him. You see, Old Giuseppe is a deaf mute."

Tony walked to the window and observed the traffic.

"*Dove Vecchio Giuseppe?*"

KING OF THE BEGGARS

Tony delved through his clothes in the hotel room. Of course he didn't plan to dress as a beggar in Rome, but he did pack a pair of old jeans, a few t-shirts and some worn out sandals for a possible beach trip. He changed into the jeans, a t-shirt with a faded silk-screened picture of James Dean and the sandals.

Before his quest to find Old Giuseppe, he popped open a can of Moretti beer from his mini refrigerator and stood out on his balcony. The same man, the amputee, he had seen the day before, sat before the entrance of the Eurostars Hotel and begged.

"My first victim," Tony said to himself and chugged the last of his beer. On his way back to the hotel from the police station, he had bought the six-pack of beer and made sure to get plenty of single euro coins as change.

Armed with a pocket full of euros and a printout of Vincenzo's mug shot, courtesy of Lieutenant Carboni, Tony hit the streets of Rome. To his surprise, another beggar had laid claim to the pavement outside his own hotel entrance. An elderly, bent over woman shook a large McDonald's coffee cup that looked as if it had been retrieved from a trash can. A little girl dressed in a dirty ragged dress clung to the woman. The woman pleaded a short phrase that Tony guessed must have meant "Money to feed my granddaughter?"

Tony dropped a euro into her cup, and she thanked him with a "God bless" phrase and a wide toothless grin.

"*Mi scuzi, senora, Dove Vecchio Giuseppe?*"

She nodded, widened her smile and repeated louder, "*Dove Vecchio Giuseppe?*"

"*Si, Si,*" Tony said, deposited another euro and asked again, "*dove Vecchio Giuseppe?*" But the reward of a euro only seemed to turn up the volume.

"*Dove Vecchio Giuseppe!*" the woman said like Paul Revere announcing that the British were coming.

Two more euros and a gathering crowd told Tony to move on. *God, I hope I have better luck down the street,* he thought and slithered toward the Eurostars Hotel. The man with the missing leg and the thin sleeping dog next to him spent his days camped just to the left of the hotel entrance.

The constant flow of people entering and exiting the hotel presented a perfect business opportunity. Most people ignored his filthy clothes, weathered face, exposed stump and lethargic mutt, but the occasional pedestrian who took pity was enough to fill the worn, dusty cap positioned near his stump with coins and bills.

Tony bent down and met the man's eyes. He patted the soft fur of the sleeping dog, and the man responded with a weak smile. After dropping a euro and some coins into the hat, he asked, "*Dove Vecchio Giuseppe?*"

"*Si,*" said the man and pointed in a general direction across and down the street. His generic indication told Tony that The King of Beggars might either be in Tony's hotel room or somewhere in Paris, France.

"*Scuzi, dove?*" Tony asked in a way that suggested, "Please be more specific."

The man looked into the sky and scratched his stubble as if he were trying to remember.

Tony dropped two more euros into his hat, and the man acted as if he were struck with an earthshaking thought and said, "*Il fiume!*"

Tony looked confused and gestured as if he were smoking a cigarette.

"No, no, *fumo. Fiume,*" the man scolded, and a made a rowing motion.

"Oh, water, aqua, the river, *Fiume Tevere?*"

"*Si, si.*"

"*Prego,*" Tony thanked him, dropped another euro into the hat and stood up.

Fiume Tevere was the river that ran through Rome. It was about a forty-minute walk, a twenty-minute public transport trip or a ten-minute drive. He glanced at his watch—two o'clock. His dinner plans with Gina and her fiancé were at seven. As much as he hated Italian city traffic and parking, he headed for his Smart car.

Fiume Tevere or the Tiber River originated more than 200 miles north of Rome and emptied into the sea about twenty miles west of it. Following the general direction of the man's pointing, Tony parked his car in a public lot near the historic bridge, Ponte Cavour.

He stood in the center of the bridge and looked down the river in both directions. Wide paved paths bordered both sides of the river below the bridge. Below him, an old man sat on a wall with his bare feet dangling in the river. His age and disheveled appearance hinted that he might be Old Giuseppe. Tony approached him, and a conversation costing him five more euros yielded that the legendary beggar was last seen rummaging for valuable trash about three kilometers or two miles west along the river.

Tony decided that walking along the path by the Tiber River provided a majestic view of Rome. The monuments and architecture loomed high above the silenced traffic above the riverbank. He pictured a night stroll with the lights illuminating each arching bridge linking the east and west sides of the city.

About three bridges down from Ponte Cavour an old man wearing a bright red t-shirt, ragged but clean black jeans, and dirty white sneakers kicked through the tall grass along the river's edge. He would on occasion bend down, pick up a glass bottle or tin can and toss it into a burlap sack he carried.

A little boy ran past Tony. The boy carried an armful of soda bottles; he deposited them into the burlap sack, and the old man nodded a thank-you.

"*Mi, scusi*, said Tony to the boy who ran by again. He pointed to the old man. *"Vecchio Giuseppe?"*

The boy didn't answer. He just darted back to the old man and gave hand gestures which included pointing at Tony. The man scrutinized Tony and then nodded to the boy.

"*Sì,*" said the boy to Tony as if he was calling a dog, and he dashed by Tony again, he presumed, to find more bottles.

Tony smiled as he approached the man.

The man neither smiled nor showed any emotion in return. He looked at Tony as if Tony were a door-to-door salesman trying to enter another man's house. His sharp blue eyes glowed deep in his leathery, weathered face. Long, thick grayish-white hair tied with a string into a short ponytail flopped just below his neck.

With a clean shave, haircut and dark suit this guy could easily look like a shrewd Wall Street banker, thought Tony.

Even though Tony knew that Old Giuseppe was a deaf mute, he accompanied his hand signals with words. It seemed to help him organize his thoughts and improvise gestures.

"I'm," he said and patted himself, "looking for," pointed to his eyes, "this man." He held up the mug shot of Vincenzo.

Old Giuseppe took the printout and stared at it for about a minute. He nodded toward Tony, stepped onto the path, and walked in a circle with an exaggerated limp.

"Yes, yes, he walked with a limp!"

He handed the picture back to Tony and continued looking for bottles and cans.

Tony stood in front of him to regain his attention, shrugged his shoulders and held his hands into the air hoping Giuseppe would interpret it to mean "Can you tell me more?" But the old man ignored him.

"Oh, sorry, I forgot," Tony said, more to himself, and pulled out a euro. This got Giuseppe's attention, but he faced Tony, shook his head and held up ten fingers.

I was right. There's a clever businessman hidden inside this seasoned beggar, he thought and gave him the ten euros plus two more to cover future costs.

Giuseppe took the money. His next gesture startled Tony. With his fist, he raised his thumb and index finger and formed the universal sign of a gun.

Tony formed his hand into a pistol, also, and said, "A gun?" He held his imaginary pistol to his head and closed his thumb symbolizing a pulled trigger and asked, "He was shot?"

Old Giuseppe shook his head in disgust. He made the gesture again and followed it up with holding one index finger up on one hand and then the index finger on the other as if he were both teaching and scolding a child for his ignorance.

It finally hit Tony. The universal hand signal for a gun was also the European gesture to mean the number two.

"Two? *Due?* Tony asked and held up his two index fingers.

Giuseppe nodded, but Tony shrugged his shoulders to communicate his question, "Two what?"

Giuseppe rummaged through a trash bin across the path for a few minutes. He approached Tony with a broken flat piece of glass and a black charred hunk of wood. At first, Tony thought the old man had had enough of this dumb American and scavenged a homemade weapon to use on him. But Giuseppe put the glass onto the blackened wood and held it to Tony's face. He had created a crude but practical mirror. He took the mug shot from Tony and held the image to the mirror. Next, using two fingers from each hand he simulated two people limping and walking away.

"My God," Tony said. "Todd found his twin, Vincenzo, and took him somewhere." He looked around in frustration as he tried to figure out how to ask when this happened. His best idea was to point to his watch and to appear puzzled.

Giuseppe responded by making an arcing motion with his arm and shivering.

"Last winter?" Tony asked, forgetting Giuseppe's deafness and his probable inability to read lips, at least in English, but he responded with a quick nod.

Tony pointed to the picture and then to his watch and asked, "Where is he now?"

Giuseppe shrugged his shoulders and went back to searching for bottles and cans.

DINNER AND A BRAWL

Tony arrived at the restaurant, *Osteria Enoteca al Bric*, a few minutes early. The drive from his hotel took only about five minutes. It wasn't far from the river and the bridge where he had encountered Old Giuseppe. Tony was eager to tell Gina what he had learned from the old beggar.

Gina and her fiancé hadn't arrived yet, so Tony took in the atmosphere of the little restaurant from the bar. Wine case lids decorated the walls of this quaint, candle-lit place. A fully stocked bar greeted patrons at the door, but the main attraction was the wine. Hundreds of bottles filled the many wine cabinets scattered throughout the restaurant. What amazed and attracted Tony most was the lack of something—tourists.

As he sipped his glass of Nero D'Avola, he peered through the opened door at the outside seating. The bald guy. There he was standing across the street and looking in at Tony. He had had enough. He set his wine glass down and headed toward the street. He would confront this guy and find out why he was following him.

Just as he reached the door, Gina and her fiancé entered and blocked his way.

"Leaving so soon? Are we that late?" asked Gina.

"No, No, I'm sorry. I thought I saw someone who—" but when Tony looked past them, the guy was gone. "Never mind. You must be Tommaso. I'm Tony, Tony Morelli, that crazy writer Gina must have told you about."

Tommaso smiled and extended a warm handshake. He reminded Tony of an Italian actor in movies from the 50s and 60s, Marcel Marceau? *No, dummy,* he scolded himself. *Marcel Marceau was a French mime. Marcello Mastroianni.* That's it. Tommaso stood eye-to-eye with Tony. His broader shoulders and thick, wavy salt-and-pepper hair reminded Tony of his handsome, warm-hearted father whom Tony idolized as a child.

The waiter spoke to Tommaso, who interpreted for Tony, "The waiter wants to know if I choose our usual table and wine selection. Only with your permission, Mr. Morelli."

"Your choice of this beautiful restaurant has earned my trust of your fine taste, and, please, call me Tony."

"*Grazie.*"

"*Prego.*"

The two men let Gina lead them to the table where the waiter stood ready to seat the party. She wore a short black dress and small spiked heels.

They are a gorgeous couple, thought Tony. He felt unusually comfortable with them. Many times when a couple entertains a third party, there is an unspoken tension. Maybe it's sexual competition or just a social uneasiness, but Gina and Tommaso appeared confident in their relationship and in themselves. They seemed eager to make Tony feel at ease. He felt like a respected visiting relative.

"So," said Tommaso and leaned forward as he sat, "Gina has been telling me you are a writer and on this quest to find this person or persons. I am intrigued. Please tell me of your adventures."

"Tommaso, let the man relax a little," Gina said, not scolding, but just as a polite etiquette reminder.

"No, No, I'm anxious to tell both of you of my progress today. Actually, it has left me a little dumbfounded of what to do next. Maybe you two have some ideas."

"I am very glad you asked," said Tommaso. "I have to confess, from what Gina tells me, I am a little jealous of the escapade you two are sharing. It seems so exciting compared to my dull banking job."

"He is too modest," Gina tells Tony. "He is a bank executive with important responsibilities and many administrators responsible to him."

The waiter brought the wine and stifled the conversation while Tommaso tasted and approved. As they sipped their wine and ate from a complimentary antipasto dish, Tony shared his "adventures" starting with Lieutenant Carboni and ending with Old Giuseppe's information about Todd finding Vincenzo.

"That's remarkable," said Gina.

"Yes, so what will you do now?" Tommaso asked.

Tony set his wine glass down, and Tommaso poured from the bottle. "Thank you. That's the problem, as I mentioned. I seem to be back to the beginning. I either have to track down Vincenzo Sagona or his half-sister, Laura Kenilworth-DiFoggio."

The waiter returned, and they ordered.

"Well," said Tony, "let's change the subject. Tell me about your wedding plans."

They both looked down at their antipasto plates and laughed, to all appearances sharing a private joke.

"The only thing we seem to agree on is the date in October, and we hope you and your girlfriend will attend," said Gina.

"If we can work out the trip, we'd love to."

"You see, Tony," Tommaso added, "I believe in the universal expression, 'opposites attract.' Gina wants a big wedding. I want a small one. She prefers the country. I like the city. It goes on and on. It is difficult to explain, but it is something that keeps us together. We love to disagree and reconcile."

Tony nodded and grinned. He knew exactly what Tommaso meant. He thought of Pauline and began to miss her. *I'll call her tonight. It'll be late here, but early enough in Chicago.*

Their dinners arrived, and, for the most part, they ate in silence.

They all passed when the dessert tray arrived, but Tommaso insisted they share his favorite dessert wine, Vin Santo, a sherry with a slight nutty flavor.

"Tony, we always finish our evening here with a walk along the river," said Tommaso. "Please don't feel you are a romantic interloper. We would love for you to join us."

"We insist," added Gina.

But Tony knew that he would be intruding, and he had a perfect excuse to decline.

"To be honest, I've had enough of walking along that river today, and seeing you two together has made me homesick for my girlfriend, Pauline. I'm going to call her as soon as I get back to the hotel and then get some needed sleep."

"We can understand that," said Gina.

"You have Gina's number, and here is my number at the bank," Tommaso said and gave him a business card. "Please don't hesitate to contact us when you need any kind of help in your search, or if you decide to finance some property in Italy, call me."

"Always the businessman," Gina teased.

They exchanged European kisses and departed.

Tony had found a parking spot on a quiet side street a few blocks west of the restaurant. He enjoyed the walk through the dark, serene residential area. Except for a few parked cars and motorbikes, the narrow brick alleyway was desolate. A dim, single-bulb porch light produced enough illumination for Tony to spot a familiar vehicle parked ahead in the darkness.

It was the dark blue sedan he had thought followed him to Gina's aunt's house a few days earlier. At least it could have been the same car. Before passing by it, he stopped and peered inside the driver's side.

The bald guy stared straight ahead as if he were waiting for someone.

"Hey, excuse me. You appear to be following me. Am I wrong?" Tony said and tapped on the window.

The man just smiled, shook his head and looked through the windshield. He opened the car door and got out in such a nonchalant, relaxed manner that Tony felt he was about to offer a rational explanation for Tony's suspicions. As soon as the car door slammed, the man's demeanor changed to a hard, professional stance.

"Sorry," he said and delivered a hard, swift punch to Tony's stomach.

Tony doubled over with pain and loss of wind. He felt the soft tingle of pepper spray in his face. The intense burning in his eyes and skin sent him cringing into a dark corner between two motorbikes.

After several minutes, the engine of the dark blue sedan purred, and the car disappeared down the street like an alley cat.

REDFORD, ELVIS & TONY

The morning sound of a truck delivering fresh bread and pastries to the café/bar across the street of Tony's hotel room awakened him. His head throbbed with a four-Tylenol headache. Ten minutes after being pepper sprayed, the burning had subsided enough to allow him to find his Smart car and to make it back to his hotel. He spent about twenty minutes splashing cold water on his face and then collapsed, fully clothed, onto his bed.

He didn't call Pauline. *Good thing,* he figured as he as he held his head and lumbered toward the bathroom, *I'd have told her all about my night and worried her sick.*

His toiletry bag always contained a bottle of Extra Strength Tylenol. He shook out four tablets. He knew it wasn't just the pepper spray that brought on his headache. Unanswered questions mounted in his head. Tony's brain didn't tolerate ambiguity. It searched for answers, even in his sleep.

Who is the bald guy? Is he really following me, or am I imagining it? Did I just scare the shit out of an innocent guy last night, and he reacted in self-defense? Was that what happened in Palermo when I thought I saw Todd? Or was it really Todd? Or Vincenzo Sagona? If the guy actually is following me, then why? How do I pick up the trail on either Laura, Vincenzo or Todd again? Should I just give up and go home?

He went to the mini-bar in his room for a cold bottle of water to wash down the Tylenol—fresh out of water bottles, plenty cans of Moretti beer. "What the hell," he said, popped open a can and talked to the caricature of a man drinking beer on the label as if it were alive. "Might as well start the day with you." He chased the tablets with a half can of beer, flopped back into bed and went to sleep.

His dream of being in the movie *All The President's Men* returned. This time he was Robert Redford's character, Bob

Woodward. In the movie, Woodward got leads on how to uncover the Watergate scandal from a guy only known as Deep Throat.

They would meet inside a dark parking garage in the dead of night. Deep Throat shielded himself behind a concrete pillar and gave Woodward hints as to who to question and what to ask. In his dream, Tony looked behind every pillar but no one was there. His head ached, and he sat down in the garage. A figure stepped from behind a cement column and walked toward him. As he got closer, the figure looked like Tommaso.

He reached into his pocket and handed Tony some Tylenol, but when Tony grabbed for the pills they turned into a business card. He tried to read the card; it was blank. "What's this?" But Tommaso had disappeared. Tony was now sitting on a beach. Elvis, wearing jeans and a denim shirt, sat beneath a palm tree and sang the title song to one of his movies to a dreamy-eyed girl.

Tony woke up. When you dream you're in a shitty Elvis film, it's time to wake up and stop the nightmare. He looked at his watch—11:20 a.m. His headache was gone. He shaved, showered, dressed and left his room for the café across the street.

People-watching ranked as one of the top European pastimes, and Tony loved it. Americans often complain about the prices at outdoor cafes. They fail to realize for what they are paying. It's not just the espresso, the pasta or anything else on the menu; it's the privilege of watching pedestrians and events unfolding on the pavement without the nuisance of a waiter rushing you along to make way for another paying customer. A patron may sip, nibble or, yes, just sit for as long as he or she wishes as long as the customer orders something.

He welcomed the escape of his problems, questions and headaches as he watched beautiful women in their short skirts, intriguing faces and mini dramas such as parents scolding their children and children scolding their parents. As he drank his cappuccino and munched on his prosciutto panini, he wanted to share the moment with Pauline, but when he reached for his cell phone, he realized he had left it in his room.

His thoughts returned to his silly dream. Who but a guy like me would dream he was Robert Redford in a movie, and what about that Elvis part? He had to laugh at himself. His humor left him when he remembered the name of the Elvis movie and title song, *Follow That Dream*. His dream about Deep Throat and Tommaso must have meant something. His subconscious was trying to send him a message . . . but what?

He called the waiter to settle his bill. All he had was a 50-euro bill, much more than his tab. When he pulled out the bill, Tommaso's business card dropped out. He picked it off the ground and stared at it. Tommaso's name, the Banca D'Italia insignia and contact information filled the center of the card—above that, an italicized quote about buying property or houses. A clip art picture of a house bordered the right side, and €, the euro symbol, bordered the left.

"Holy shit. That's it. Here, keep the change," he said to a rather confused-looking waiter, gave him the 50-euro bill and ran back to his hotel.

FOLLOW THAT DREAM

"I've gotta follow that dream wherever that dream may lead me . . . " Tony sang those lyrics as he dialed Gina's number from the phone in his hotel room. In his dream, Elvis or his subconscious were telling him that his *All The President's Men* dream had meaning, and he had figured it out at last.

"*Pronto?*"

"Gina, it's Tony. Did the movie *All The President's Men* ever play here in Italy back in the 70s or 80s?"

"What are you talking about?"

"It's about the Watergate scandal in America, the one that led to President Nixon's resignation. Anyway, this guy named Deep Throat gives clues to these two reporters, and his main advice is 'follow the money.' Get it?"

"Keep talking until you start making some sense."

"If Todd embezzled millions of dollars from the mob and ran to Europe, he must have done something with it. He either invested it or put it in a bank. It's not likely that he'd carry all that cash for long. Look, Tommaso gave me his card and said he wanted to help us. I don't know if he was just being polite, or if I would be too bold to ask him, so I was wondering if you thought it would be a good idea to ask him if he had any ideas on how to track the money."

Gina's momentary pause was enough to make Tony anxious. Maybe this was another dead end.

"No."

"No?"

"I mean, no, he was not just being polite. He would love to help, but sometimes his work gets very complicated, and he can't take the time. Let me call him, and I'll get right back to you."

"Great."

Within in two minutes, she called back.

Too quick. Not a good sign.

"Bad news?" Tony asked instead of "*Pronto*" or "Hello."

"Not really. He is in a meeting but will call back when it is over."

Tony dreaded his least favorite pastime, waiting all day for a call.

"Fine. Do you have my cell phone number?"

"Yes, it is on my cell phone as well as your hotel room telephone number."

"Good. I think I'll get out of this stuffy room and do some sightseeing."

"Very good. Can I help with any suggestions or directions?"

"No, thanks, Gina. I think I know exactly what I need to see."

He hung up and picked up his laminated street map of Rome.

*****

It was only a ten minute walk down Via Nazionale from his hotel to the Victor Emmanuel Monument, where, according to news sources, Todd Kenilworth "leaped from the nearly eighty meter high panoramic observation deck" and died. Tony stood at street level and looked up at the structure from the first set of white cement stairs that led toward the monument.

It was a full city block wide. Four tiers of these stairs led tourists up to a massive walkway. To the right and left of the main entrance were two fountains, representations of the two seas that border Italy. At the center of the monument was the equestrian statue of Victor Emmanuel, the 'Father of the Nation'. Tony knew little about the statue or Victor Emmanuel. He really wanted to know if there was any significance in Todd or whoever choosing this place as his suicide site.

Rather than do honest research, he decided to take the independent tourist's shortcut, eavesdrop on a tour guide's lecture to a paying tour group. He chose to listen to a beautiful statuesque Italian tour guide speaking with a British accent to a group of American-looking senior vacationers who had just disembarked from a boxcar-and-a-half sized air-conditioned bus. She stood on the third step leading up to the statue and held a closed umbrella pointed toward the sky, the universal method tour guides used to gather their flocks. An aging Italian man, not with the group, joined Tony listening in on the oration.

"Victor Emmanuel II lived from 1820–78. He is considered to be the first king of a united Italy from 1861-1878. He was opposed to constitutionalism and believed in absolute royal authority, but retained the constitution, or Statuto, granted by his father in 1848. His unification of Italy included two major conquests. He conquered and annexed Sicily and defeated the Papal army, costing him the Pope's excommunication.

He then moved the capitol to Rome. The Monument to Victor Emanuel II is also known as the Altare della Patria or the Altar of the Nation. You will notice that it is decorated with numerous allegorical statues, reliefs and murals, which artists from all over Italy created. The colossal equestrian statue of Victor Emmanuel is known also as the 'Father of the Nation'. It is the work of sculptor Enrico Chiaradia. It weighs fifty tons and measures twelve meters long, which would be about thirty-nine feet. It rests on a pedestal decorated with allegorical reliefs representing Italian cities.

Just above us and at the foot of the statue is the Tomb of the Unknown Soldier, inaugurated in 1921. Honor guards selected from the marine, infantry and air divisions, stand on guard here twenty-four hours."

Like lemmings, they followed her umbrella toward the observation deck farther away.

Tony and his fellow aged Italian eavesdropper stood staring at the huge sculpture. Tony could not draw a correlation linking anything the guide had said with the reason Todd might have chosen this place to kill himself.

"*Mi scusi. Parli inglese?*" Tony asked the old man.

"*Si.* Yes."

"Do you live here in Rome?"

"Yes."

"This may sound like a silly question, but a friend of mine chose this area to take his own life, to kill himself, last winter. Have other people done that here? I mean, is there any connection with this statue and death?"

The man gazed at the statue for a minute.

"No, I don't think so. But I can tell you this. We Romans hate this ugly thing. We call it *ridicolo torta di compleanno*, the ridiculous wedding or birthday cake."

The old man turned and walked away.

Tony stepped back to get a broader look.

Damn, it does look like a wedding or birthday cake.

Behind the statute were fifty-foot pillars with two bronze statues framing them on either side representing winged victors. The pillars supported the observation deck that spanned half a city block between the victory statues.

Tony walked behind the base of the mammoth-sized pillars to the observation deck elevator. He wondered if Todd had stood in line and paid the seven euros to ride the elevator, or if he climbed one of the two stairwells beneath the victory statues only to jump to his death.

The elevator brought Tony and about a dozen other people to the top. Tourists crowded the deck, took pictures, "oohed" and "aahed" at the magnificent views of The Colosseum and other old Roman ruins and sites.

It would have been easy for Todd to maneuver over the four-foot railing and to vault over the ornate flower petal shaped edge, but would he have done so with all these tourists up here and down below, he wondered? He recalled some details from the news clippings. *No, it was February, off-season—a dreary day, bad for picture taking, and, I think, it was late in the day, probably near closing time.*

Even though his elevator ticket was good for the ride down, he headed for one of the big brown wooden doors at the base of each winged victory statue that opened to a stairwell. Just as he pulled the door open, his cell phone rang.

It must be Gina with either good or bad news. He released the door handle and reached for his phone.

BAD NEWS, GOOD NEWS

"Tommaso said for us to meet him at Bar Gianicolo in fifteen minutes," Gina said. "Where are you right now?"

"I'm on the observation deck of the Victor Emmanuel Monument. Did he find anything out?" Tony said.

"He did not say, just, 'I have both bad and good news.' It will take you about ten or fifteen minutes to drive there. It is on the other side of the river."

"I don't have my car, so I'll either have to walk, take a bus or go back to my hotel to get my car."

"All those ways will take too much time. I'll pick you up in front of the monument in less than five minutes."

"But—"

She hung up.

*****

It was as Tony had feared. Gina in her little Vespa motorbike zoomed toward the monument steps where he waited. If he had gotten over feeling foolish driving his six-foot body around in his less that five-foot Smart car, he would never get over the ludicrous image of himself riding on the back of this toy-like motorcycle with petite Gina driving.

"Here, you have to wear this," said Gina and handed him a helmet.

"Well, when in Rome. . ." said Tony and squeezed his head into the undersized pink helmet that covered only the top half of his ears.

Gina choked back a laugh, turned her head and mounted her bike.

Tony squatted onto the extended back of the seat. He pictured himself in the movie, *Easy Rider*—the scene where the nerdy lawyer that Jack Nicholson played rides on the back of the Harley driven by cool looking Peter Fonda. Jack wore a football helmet and flapped his arms like a gull.

Tony mimicked the flapping Jack character and sang the lyrics, "Born to be w-i-i-l-d . . ." as they zipped and swerved through the narrow Roman side streets.

She parked in front of Bar Gianicolo and peeled off her helmet. When she turned around, Tony was still trying to pry his pink helmet off his ears and head. This time she didn't try to hide her amusement. She threw back her head and laughed.

"Sorry," she said.

"No you're not. Now I know how an elephant turd must feel if it were shat from a mouse's ass."

This time they both chuckled.

Whenever Gina laughed her hair dangled around her delicate bare shoulders. Her full lips parted. Tony wondered what it would be like to kiss her. He felt himself starting to fall for her; it scared him, because he also loved Pauline and missed her more each day.

"So, did you enjoy the view from the observation deck at the Victor Emmanuel Monument?"

"Yes, but that's not why it intrigued me," Tony answered, and they sat at one of the outdoor tables with an umbrella outside the bar/café.

"*Che cosa possoottenere per voi?*" asked a waiter dressed in a coat and tie. He had emerged from inside Bar Gianicolo via a hanging beaded doorway.

Gina spoke a few words to him, and he went back inside.

"I told him we were waiting for another person, but we would order shortly," she said to Tony. "Now, you said something intrigued you today?"

"Yes, the place where your cousin allegedly committed suicide—"

"Excuse me, my English is pretty good, but this word, 'allegedly,' is foreign to me."

Tony fumbled for a synonym. "It means . . . questionable . . . maybe not proven. In this case, it means several things. First of all, was it suicide or did someone kill him? Second, who was it? Was it Todd? Could it have been Vincenzo or maybe someone else? Did one of them kill the other?"

"You still have not answered my question. What intrigued you?"

"Yes, I have. It's the place . . . and the time. It was perfect for either a suicide or a homicide."

"Am I late?"

It was Tommaso. While Gina and Tony looked somewhat windblown and weathered from the wild Vespa ride, Tommaso appeared fresh, well-groomed and professional in a dark Armani suit.

"No," Tony said, stood and shook his hand. "We literally just blew in."

The waiter returned. Tommaso ordered an espresso and apologized for not drinking something alcoholic because he still had much work to do at the bank. He encouraged the others to order whatever they wanted; it was on his bank's tab. Tony ordered a cold beer, and Gina requested carbonated mineral water and a glass of Nero D'Avola wine.

"I suppose both of you are anxious to hear what I discovered," said Tommaso as he retrieved a file folder from his briefcase. He placed it in front of him and folded his hands over it.

Tony and Gina sat forward like little children waiting to hear a story from their daddy.

"I had my assistant check on the names that Gina gave to me." He read from notes he had scribbled on the folder's cover, "Todd Kenilworth, Laura Kenilworth-DiFoggio, and Vincenzo Sagona. I even had her try different combinations of first and last names. The bad news, the names are not listed as clients from any Italian bank or its subsidiaries in other countries."

"So," said Tony, "it means Todd Kenilworth either didn't steal millions from the mob, or he has it hidden somewhere other than a bank."

"Perhaps," said Tommaso, "but more likely he could have done what many rich Americans do. He deposited it in a Swiss bank where safety and confidentiality are well-known throughout the world."

"Then, if he took this money, we can never find out what he did with it," said Gina.

"We are only unable to find out where he deposited that much money, not necessarily where he may have spent it."

Daddy had gotten to the story's climax and little Tony and Gina leaned in closer.

"The good news, my anxious children, is that our laws here in Italy about the exchange of property are similar in some ways as yours, Tony, in the United States. When someone buys real estate property in Italy it is, as you call it in America, 'public record.' Here is what we found." He pulled two photocopies of a document with a section circled. "Gina, my dear, for Tony's benefit, would you tell him the essence of the passage."

Gina, her mouth open as if in some kind of disbelief, scanned the paragraph and then looked into Tony's eyes. "It says that in April of this year, one Vincenzo Sagona purchased a villa in Cefalù within the Palermo region for three million euros."

The drinks arrived, and Tony needed one.

PART III:

DÉJÀ VU

CEFALÙ

"It's about time you called," said Pauline. "I was beginning to think you were having another romantic Italian affair, but this time with someone else."

Tony laughed but felt guilty about his recent attraction to Gina. He could never fall out of love with Pauline. At the same time, he caught himself having sexual fantasies about Gina.

"We—meaning Gina, her fiancé and I—are on to something." He told her about his encounters with Carboni and Old Giuseppe and his discoveries about the existence of Vincenzo Sagona and the property he bought in Cefalù.

"So what's your next move?" asked Pauline.

"I'm going to Sicily to find out if Vincenzo Sagona is either Vincenzo Sagona, Todd Kenilworth or someone else. Have the police been able to tie him or Laura to the car bombing yet?"

"I don't know. I haven't heard anything since they came looking for you after you left. Isn't this extended stay and the Sicily trip getting a little expensive?"

"Ah, that's the beauty of it. This investigation may end up with evidence of bank or property fraud. That's part of Tommaso's, that's Gina's fiancé's, work. He buys government-confiscated property for his bank at auction prices, and his bank finances loans for buyers. He's become so intrigued with this story that his employer, Banca D'Italia, is paying the expenses.

"Actually, it's a short plane shuttle ride to Palermo and a forty-five minute drive from there to Cefalù. If I leave early enough, I can make the trip in a day. That way I can feel less guilty about charging Tommaso's bank with an overnight business trip. Plus, I'll be back in my Rome hotel bed at night and having phone sex with a provocative, red-headed blues singer."

"Well, just be careful and come back soon. I miss the hell out of you."

"I miss you, too. Love you."

"I love you, too."

Tony felt guiltier after he had hung up. *I didn't lie to her, but is not telling the whole truth lying?* What is the truth? He didn't mention the bald guy, but that wasn't the source of his guilty conscience. No, knowledge of his being followed would have just worried her. He knew what he had left out; he wasn't going to Sicily alone. Gina would be with him.

*****

Tommaso drove Gina and Tony to the airport. In a technical sense, Banca D'Italia employed all three. Tommaso, Executive Administrator of Property and Finance, had subcontracted Gina and Tony to investigate the ownership of property which one Vincenzo Sagona had purchased. If the owner turned out to be anyone but Vincenzo, the government would confiscate the property, and charge the owner with fraud. Banca D'Italia could attain the property through Tommaso's connections.

The plan was that Gina and Tony would confront the owner on the true premise that Gina was Vincenzo's cousin and wished to meet him, and Tony was an American friend of the family. They could return that same day.

There are several ways to get to Palermo from Rome. Romantics take the night train or the ferry. People with patience and pluck, drive the nearly 600 miles and discover that the only worse drivers than Romans are Sicilians. Business travelers used to be the only people that flew, but cheap commuter flights take less than an hour, so most people choose to fly.

Tommaso dropped them off at the departure gate of EasyJet Airlines.

"Call me as soon as you know something," He said to both of them while handing a folder of travel vouchers to Gina.

Gina kissed him through the driver's side window, and he drove away. An awkward silence settled between them that Tony didn't quite comprehend. After all, they had been alone together several times since their first meeting.

"Shall we go, Mr. Sherlock Holmes?" Gina said and took Tony's arm.

"Lead the way, Dr. Watson."

The silence was broken.

Tommaso had arranged for the car rental of a Mercedes C250 coupe. Tony felt a little disappointed that it wasn't a little, cheap Smart car. He had gotten accustomed to the little vehicle the same way one gets used to wearing a comfortable pair of jeans. It didn't matter because Gina insisted on driving.

"I'm always zipping around in my little Vespa, and Tommaso drives the car. I never get the chance to drive such a luxury thing."

Tony soon learned why Tommaso did most of the driving. Gina drove like a typical Italian—flat out fast with little regard for any traffic laws, assuming there were any in Sicily.

As they drove the less-than fifty-mile distance between Palermo and Cefalù, Tony realized that the man who hit him in the jaw several weeks ago had to have been the same guy who lived in this house. It would have been a short trip from Cefalù by car, bus or train to the library where Tony had spoken in Palermo.

Was it Todd or Vincenzo?

Gina pulled off the main highway, A20, and said, "You must see the Cefalù coastline before we look for this house."

So far Tony was unimpressed. He had heard that Cefalù was this beautiful resort town like the French Riviera, but all he saw from the highway was farmland. Gina's driving went from reckless to reticent. It was the only way to absorb the magnificent sandy seashore, first desolate and serene, then crowded and active.

Each of the commercial beaches on the coastal side of the road displayed its unique umbrella colors. Neon flashing hotel signs and long stretches of outdoor restaurants with awnings sparkling in the bright sunlight and owners pitching their menus beckoned attention from the other side.

"This is exciting," said Tony. "Damn, we should have brought swimwear."

"We did," said Gina and pointed to her large travel bag.

"For me, too?"

"I bought Tommaso an extra pair of swim trunks for occasions like this."

Tony tried to hide his distaste of wearing another man's swim trunks, but his expression must have caught Gina's eye."

"Do not worry, Mr. Modest Tony Morelli. They have never been worn, and you may keep them if you like. There is plenty of time for play. Let us see if we can find this three million euro villa first."

"According to the GPS, it's farther down the coast and away from the central city."

The coastal road ended at a stone stairway leading to another level of the city.

"We need to go back onto the main city street to the right. Up those stairs is the pedestrian walkway with some wonderful shops and restaurants. We can visit there later, also."

Taking the scenic route must have thrown the GPS off. It recalculated the trip along SS113, a coastal highway, for about seven kilometers until they reached a place called Lido Babaja.

"You have reached your destination," said the GPS lady.

It was a private beach, a hotel and a restaurant.

"Could this be it?" asked Tony.

"I don't know. Let's ask at the restaurant."

The two-story hotel and restaurant occupied the same stucco, terra cotta roof building. They entered from the front and could see that the back of the restaurant had no wall and led to a terrace of tables overlooking the beach. It hadn't opened for lunch yet. A thin, balding man wearing a sleeveless t-shirt, white pants and an apron worked with a teen-aged girl setting tables on the terrace.

"*Buongiorno, sedere. Apriamopresto*," he said and motioned for them to come outside and be seated, despite the early time.

"*Mi scusi*," said Gina.

They approached the man on the terrace, and Gina began a lengthy animated conversation with him. Several times he pointed to a peninsula far down the beach with a steep, rocky hillside and a boat dock between the hotel beach and the peninsula. The conversation ended with Gina motioning for Tony to sit down and the girl serving them wine, water, fresh bread, cheese and olive oil.

"Well, don't leave me in suspense," said Tony as the girl poured the water and wine.

"Better drink some wine first," Gina said and tore off a piece of bread.

SIGNOR SAGONA

"Do you see that piece of land sticking out into the sea?" Gina asked Tony and pointed to the peninsula.

"Yes."

"He lives on the other side of those hills."

"Okay, let's go."

"It is impossible to get there—at least by car."

"So, how does one get there?"

"Either by walking the shoreline on those fucking rocks, which I refuse to do in these shoes or my bare feet, or by boat."

It was the first time Tony had heard Gina swear. It didn't become her, not that he thought she was too pure, but it just didn't fit the image he had of her. "Well, how the fuck does the owner get to his house?"

"Look down the shoreline."

About a quarter mile down the beach and toward the peninsula, a long cement dock jutted into the water. Several small yachts tied to the dock bobbed with the waves.

"He owns one of those boats."

The girl poured each another glass of wine and asked if they wanted to order. The restaurant had opened. They both declined.

"If one of those boats is his, then he is not home. So, where is he, and more importantly, who is he?"

"I asked him. He said no one knows much about the man. The owner has only lived there a few months and does not speak to anyone. He is only known as Signor Sagona and walks with a limp. His boat has been docked there for a few days."

"What do we do now?"

"The man says his son runs a water taxi/charter boat/shoreline tour from that dock. He will take us to Signor Sagona's villa."

"Great. Let's go."

"The son is out on a fishing charter and won't be back until late afternoon."

"What do we do in the meantime?"

Gina gulped down her wine, spread out her arms and smiled like a happy child. "We go swimming!"

Tony scanned the rocky beach. "I thought you didn't like these 'fucking rocks' as you called them."

"Not here, silly Morelli, back at the resort area. Drink up. We are losing valuable beach time."

*****

Lido Apollo with its signature blue and white striped umbrellas appeared to be the most popular of the many commercial beaches along Lungomare Giuseppe Giardina, the resort area they had visited earlier. Twenty euros bought them the use of two cabanas, two cushioned lounge chairs under an umbrella with an attached table and a complimentary drink at the bar/restaurant.

Tony had prayed that Tommaso's trunks weren't Speedos, and his prayers were answered. The blue, baggy-style surfer trunks were a perfect fit. He dug his toes into the warm, pale sand and took in the atmosphere while he waited for Gina to finish dressing in her cabana. The hot Sicilian sun baked his olive skin, but the fresh sea breeze felt like a spray of cool lotion.

The wooden door of Gina's cabana door creaked open. Her red and white small-checkered bikini looked almost pink at a distance. It accentuated the smooth, brown curves of her breasts, hips and legs. *Tommaso, what a lucky man*, he thought. She grabbed the towels from him.

"*Andiamo*, let's go. We are wasting time," she said and ran toward an unoccupied umbrella-table-and-chairs set, but she didn't stop. She threw the towels and her bag of belongings onto a chair and sprinted toward the water.

Tony did the same.

When the water was knee-deep, Gina dove forward as if the sandy bottom was a springboard, and she swam smooth strokes toward deeper water. Tony executed a less graceful dive and followed. An unexpected wave caught her by surprise, and she breathed in some water. She stood—the water up to her neck—and coughed. Tony swam toward her and held her by her shoulders.

"Are you okay?"

She nodded but continued to choke. She put her hands onto his shoulders to steady herself. Her arms slid around his neck, and his dropped to her waist. He felt her thighs next to his and became aroused. As if by instinct, their eyes closed, and they shared a long passionate kiss. It ended with them touching foreheads and Gina said, "Tony, what are we doing?"

"I don't know. Is it wrong?"

"No, it is natural, but it may cause some hurt."

"I could never stop loving Pauline."

"And I love Tommaso. Those aren't the people that will get hurt."

"Then, who?"

"Us, our relationship."

Tony looked confused. He had been thinking with his libido, not his brain.

Gina stepped back and held Tony's hands. "Tony, Tony, we have established a close bond. I don't know what to call it—friendship, siblings, I don't know. If we become lovers, we may never have that again. Do you want to risk it?"

Tony didn't answer. He hadn't thought of that. *Italians are so ahead of us Americans when it comes to love and so many other things.*

"Well, I do not," she said, kissed him on the mouth and swam to shore.

*****

The ride back to Lido Babaja differed from the previous visit. Tony took the wheel. He wanted to show Gina how Americans drove, with caution and courtesy. An important shift had occurred, the atmosphere between them had changed; it was more open, relaxed. Their sexual tension had been resolved, and their true respective love interests, Pauline and Tommaso, renewed.

"Do all Americans drive the way you do?" Gina asked as they entered the parkway in front of the hotel/restaurant at Lido Babaja.

"Only Americans who don't like spending time in traffic court and paying too much money for car insurance."

"Then I must conclude that those Americans drive too slowly, like old ladies."

"Better to drive like a living old lady than a crazy one tempting death."

Gina put her thumb over the mouth of her bottle of Diet Coke, shook it and sprayed Tony in the face.

"Hey, that's not fair," said Tony and turned his attention toward finding a parking spot. "Watch this magic trick." He found a tight space and pulled next to the car in front of it. Without touching the brake pedal, he backed the car into the space.

"So where is the magic?"

"It's called parallel parking. I never see Italians do it. If they see a tight parking space, they just stab the front end into it and let the rear end stick out into traffic."

"This 'parallel parking' is a waste of time," Gina said and opened her door.

Tony threw back his head and laughed.

As soon as they stepped inside the restaurant, the thin proprietor recognized them. This time, he wore a white sport coat and tie and acted as the host. He held his finger up as a signal to wait and then scurried through the room now half full of patrons dressed in casual summer attire. When he reached the terrace, he yelled something over the wall and toward the beach.

In an instant, a young man hurdled over the stone wall like a track star and faced the owner. As they engaged in conversation, they looked like mirror images separated only by time and clothes. The younger man had a thick crop of black hair and wore long, flowered beach trunks, sandals and a white shirt with the sleeves rolled up. He nodded, smiled as the older man spoke and gave him an okay sign that ended the talk.

His smile seemed to get broader and broader as he bolted through the restaurant toward Gina and Tony.

"My father tells me one of you is American and both of you want to go to Signor Sagona's house." He spoke to both of them, but his eyes focused only on Gina.

"Yes," said Tony.

"Good, I can practice my English on you. Now, can I interest you in a romantic sunset cruise, a tour of the coastline or maybe a fishing trip—all half-price with the cost of your service today. Courtesy of Carlo's Taxi Service."

"No, thank you," said Gina, "just the round trip now."

"No problem," said Carlo, his engaging smile and enthusiasm not wavering. "Follow me."

They followed him onto the parkway and into his yellow, open—no doors, windows or roof—Jeep Wrangler. He was already in third gear before he left his parking spot. The Jeep skidded right onto a single lane gravel path along the two-lane road that connected the hotel with the main *strada*.

Tony realized that the only thing scarier than riding with a crazy Italian driver on a road in Italy is riding with a crazy Italian driver in an off-road vehicle off a road. His white knuckles clutching the roll bar matched his pale face as he closed his eyes and prayed that no one came from the opposite direction.

The Jeep came to an abrupt halt.

Tony opened his eyes. The gravel dust cloud settled. They were in a small, circular crushed-stone lot at the base of the long cement pier visible from the hotel terrace. Only two other cars occupied space near the water. They walked the length of the dock. Only a few slips were vacant. On each side of the pier, small but sleek yachts tied to iron moorings stood rigid against the late afternoon tide that crashed at the shore.

He wondered which vessel belonged to Signor Sagona, but didn't think to ask until they reached the end of the dock where Carlo's taxi boat bobbed and twisted like a cork with each wave.

"Which one belongs to Signor Sagona, Carlo?"

Carlo had already jumped onto the bow and extended a hand to help Gina and then Tony aboard. "It is at the beginning. I'll show you when we return."

The bow had railings on both sides to steady passengers' short walk to four steps that led down into the shallow hollow of the boat. Two long benches on each side of the wall allowed commuters to sit and view the sea and coastline over the side. Fishing gear, rods and bait pails filled the area in the rear. A white canopy stretched over the thirty-foot length of the boat with a banner that read: CARLO'S TAXI ACQUA.

Carlo's wild driving on the road did not extend to the sea. He backed his boat from the dock as if he were guiding a feeble loved one through a crowd. When the vessel seemed to be a safe distance from the few rock formations that remained in these deep waters, he angled it parallel to the peninsula and motored against the current and out to sea. The deafening hum of the engine squelched any dialogue softer than yelling.

Signor Sagona's villa came into view as soon as they were about fifty yards beyond the peninsula. Somehow, it looked both garish and plain. A high stone wall that looked centuries old with a rusty metal railing on top extended along the shore as if protecting the villa. Behind the wall, it looked like someone had stacked huge white building blocks with windows on top of each other, erratic like the way a baby would stack toy blocks. A cement dock, much like the one they had just left, extended from the wall.

Carlo cut the engine to idle speed and motioned for them to come forward. Above the engine's low hum he spoke. "That wall is all that is left of a fifteenth century castle. About twelve or fifteen years ago a very rich Frenchman had the castle destroyed. He had that very ugly villa built for his young starlet mistress, at her, what is the English word?"

After a short pause, Tony offered, "Specifications?"

"Yes, specifications. After only one or two years, he discovered she was having affairs and wild parties, so he had her thrown out. It had been vacant for maybe ten or more years until Signor Sagona bought it not too many months ago. No one knows anything about him. A caretaker he brought from Rome lives there with him. He speaks English, Italian and some other language, but mainly he just says, 'Signor Sagona does not wish to be disturbed' whenever he speaks."

As Carlo steered closer to the dock, Gina said to Tony, "Look, there are no other boats and only two spaces to dock a boat. I am a little frightened. We should make sure Carlo waits for us."

"Carlo, wait for us please," said Tony.

"Of course, as long as your visit is short. This is not like America. Our taxis do not have. . . what do you call them, meters?"

"Yes, your English is very good."

Carlo seemed honored by Tony's compliment as he tied his boat to the moor and helped them onto the dock.

Tony and Gina walked along the dock to the shore and ascended a set of stairs to the right of the wall leading to a brick terrace. Pillars supported the villa that towered above the wall and provided shade for a patio furnished with white wicker outdoor furniture.

A tall, handsome man in his late forties or early fifties stood at the top of the stairs as if he had been expecting them. He wore a bright yellow knit Polo shirt, brilliant white cotton slacks and matching white boat shoes and no socks. His slicked-back dyed black hair, tan skin and prominent nose gave him the look of a rich Mafia don.

"*Buongiorno, Come posso aiutarla?*" he asked with a warm smile, but his body guarded them from stepping onto the patio.

"*Buongiorno. Scusi,*" said Gina, "for the benefit of my American friend, can we speak in English?"

"Yes, I am quite fluent with several languages," he answered with a slight English accent.

"Now, what can I do for you?"

"We are here to see Signor Sagona."

"Is he expecting you?"

"I do not think so, but I think he would like to see us."

"Who should I say wants to see him?"

"My name is Gina Sagona. I believe we are cousins. This man is Tony. He is visiting, and, shall we say, he is a family friend."

"I see. Unfortunately, Signor Sagona is not here. He is in Rome on business."

They had guessed by seeing his yacht docked at the other pier that he wasn't at home, but hoped he was just in town or nearby.

"When do you expect him to return?" asked Tony.

"Not until late tomorrow afternoon."

"Then, we would like to make an appointment to see him then," said Gina.

"I will inform him of your intentions."

An awkward silence followed. The man neither offered further information about Signor Sagona or himself, nor extended hospitality beyond the stairs, so they left.

"I thought we had a flight booked back to Rome tonight," said Tony.

"We do, but let me call Tommaso and see what he can do."

Tony walked back to the boat and let Gina talk in private to her fiancé.

Before Carlo could start the noisy engine, Gina joined them on the boat and said to Tony, "Tommaso is making arrangements for us to stay at Hotel Riva Del Sole in town where his bank books business travel. We can make last minute flight arrangements after we meet with this Signor Sagona."

As soon as they docked, Tony paid Carlo and gave him a generous tip. He remembered to ask, "Now which boat belongs to Signor Sagona?"

"It is on the right side, third space from the shore."

Tony and Gina walked to the yacht while Carlo tended to the maintenance of his boat.

The yacht appeared to be about thirty-five or forty feet in length and three levels high with a retractable diving board hanging over the rear sundeck. They stepped onto the bow and prepared to search it, but Carlo interrupted them running and yelling down the pier.

"Signor Tony, there is an emergency phone call for you at the hotel. My father just sent a text message."

Tony jumped from the yacht and ran to the Jeep.

TORCIA ELETTRICA

Carlo couldn't drive fast enough for Tony. The Jeep sprayed gravel behind them, and Tony kept his eyes wide open. If he closed them, he saw Pauline sprawled out on the side of the road again, her hair and face singed. *What happened? What's this emergency call?*

Tony was out of the Jeep even before Carlo brought it to an abrupt stop at the curb. Carlo's father handed Tony a local number to call. Without asking permission, he called the number from the restaurant reception desk.

"*Pronto?*"

"My name is Tony Morelli. Someone left a message for me at this number." It didn't even occur to him whether or not the other party spoke English, but after a short pause the person spoke.

"Mr. Morelli, I called my employer as soon as you and your lady friend departed. He informed me that he will not be returning tomorrow. Furthermore, he does not wish to meet with you. In fact, sir, if you are seen on the premises, I am to call the local *polizia* and have you arrested."

"But why—"

He hung up.

Tony relayed the news to Gina and ended with, "Well, here we are again, back to square one. Any ideas?"

"Yes, we eat. I'm starving."

They took a table on the terrace overlooking the beach. A few twilight swimmers bathed in the water off the rocky shore. They, of course, ordered a bottle of Nero D'Avola wine. Tony ordered black squid ink pasta and Gina, pesto lasagna.

"So let us go to this 'square one' you mentioned. Maybe we should go back to the beginning and review what we know and do not know. We are looking for Vincenzo Sagona. He would be my cousin. I am interested in my family tree. What is your interest in him?"

"He is the twin brother of a guy I knew from my childhood, Todd Kenilworth—a guy I thought I saw in Palermo last month on my book tour. When I confronted him, he knocked me out, similar to the treatment we got from this mysterious Signor Sagona. Being a writer, I smell a possible story for a book or essay.

"My research tells me Todd committed suicide in Rome. Why? His sister tells me he was despondent over a broken marriage and his father's death, but Todd's ex has a different more plausible theory. Todd and his brother-in-law may have embezzled millions from the mob when his brother-in-law died in the 9/11 tragedy, which possibly left a share to his wife, Todd's sister.

"A newspaper story may have tipped off the mob that Todd had the money. A short time thereafter, Todd and his sister, Laura, came to Italy, and he jumps from the Victor Emmanuel Monument."

They toasted their first glass of wine. Gina asked, "So what is the interest in finding his sister, Laura?"

"At this point, I want to find her even more than I want to find out the truth about Todd and Vincenzo. Yes, she may lead me to what happened, and a good story, but my interest is personal. After I confronted her about my interest in writing about her brother, she threw me out of her house and a few days later a bomb was planted in my car; it nearly killed the love of my life, Pauline.

"They caught the guy who planted the bomb, and he has ties to Todd. The police and I suspect that Laura hired him, and they're trying to build a case around it. It won't do any good if they can't find her. If I find her, I can notify American law enforcement and the Italian authorities and expedite the extradition process."

Their dinners arrived.

"How can you eat black spaghetti?" asked Gina.

"The same way you can eat green lasagna."

They ate in silence. A full moon provided enough light to watch white water crash against the jagged shore. Below the glow from the harbor light at the end of the pier, Carlo's water taxi plunged and climbed with each dip and swell of the waves.

"I have an idea," Gina said and gulped down her wine. "Finish your wine and pay the bill."

"Yessum, Miss Gina."

He guzzled and hailed the waiter.

Gina jumped into the driver's seat of the Mercedes and told Tony to buckle his safety belt and prepare for a wild ride. "Do you remember what we were doing when Carlo gave you that emergency message?"

"No."

The wine had fogged Tony's short-term memory.

"We were about to search Signor Sagona's yacht. Wait. It is too dark. Go ask in the hotel if we might borrow a flashlight. The word in Italian is *torcia elettrica*."

He returned, shined the light in her face and said with a playful, menacing voice, "*Torcia elettrica*."

"Sober up, please."

The short ride to the dock did just that. Gina's reckless driving made Carlo's chauffeuring seem like a little old lady driving to church.

Tony led with the flashlight beam, guiding them to the boat. From the bow, they climbed to the top platform and searched all three levels. The yacht was beautiful and spotless, too spotless. There were no personal items or documents onboard. It looked pristine enough to be on a boat dealer's lot waiting to be sold. Gina flopped onto a cushioned lounge chair on the rear sunbathing deck.

Tony laid the retractable diving board over the side. He walked toward the end and felt it bounce above the water. The light from the *torcia elettrica* illuminated writing on the rear of the boat. The freshly painted boat's name reflected in bright pink lettering: BECKY'S DREAM.

Tony almost fell into the water.

FINEZZE

"Tell me all about the Italian school system," Tony said as he jumped from the diving board onto the sun deck. He pulled a white plastic chair close to Gina who reclined in the lounge chair and sat next to her. She appeared to enjoy lying on this outdoor recliner and gazing at the stars. The day's activities had taken a toll on her. She looked at Tony as if he were a talking dog and said, "What in the hell are you asking me?"

"You grew up and were educated in Sicily, but you've lived in Rome for some time now. I want to know all about the Italian school system."

She closed her eyes and didn't even ask why he wanted to know. She seemed too tired to care and surrendered to his mysterious inquisition. "What do you want to know?"

"First, do you have compulsory education in Italy?"

"What is that?"

"Are kids required to be in school by law?"

"Yes, parents must have their children between the ages of six and sixteen enrolled in a public or private school."

"Okay, in America, most schools are not in session during the summer. What about here?"

"It is the same here. The regular school year is September through June."

Tony looked discouraged when he heard this and then asked, "What do you mean by 'regular?' I mean, do any kids attend school in the summer?"

"Of course. If a child needs to catch up, there are summer sessions."

"Now, let's say I came here from a foreign country, in late summer. I intended to stay in Italy for a long time, maybe even become a citizen, would I need to register my kid for school?"

"I know all Italian citizens must have their children registered in a school at least sixty days before the start of the next school year. I must assume that applies to foreigners applying for citizenship or a long stay. It is already August. The Italian school year starts in just a few weeks." Gina sat up. Her fatigue disappeared, and she looked curious. "What are you thinking?"

"I'm thinking we've been following the wrong people, adults, especially adults motivated to hide. Adults can easily change their names and disguise themselves if they want to. It's harder to alter a kid's identity for school registration. I'm sure Italian schools require inoculation records, transcripts and all the bureaucratic crap to enroll children in an Italian school, just like American schools. Laura brought her fourteen-year old daughter over here, and from what I gathered from the real estate agent selling their house in the U.S., she left kicking and screaming. That might work to our advantage down the road."

"Tony, are you suggesting we check all the . . . did you say she was fourteen?"

He nodded.

"We would have to check all the public and private *scuola secondaria di secondo grado or scuola superiore.* There must be hundreds in the Roman region alone. Even if we checked all of them they probably would not give us confidential. . . "

She stopped talking and held up her hand. "Wait. If she does not speak Italian and does not cherish being in Italy but would rather be with her American friends, it is not likely her mother would enroll her into an Italian school. There is what is called RISA, Rome International School Association. They are schools designed for foreign students. Her mother would probably register her in a RISA school. There are several of them, but fewer than Italian schools. We still have the problem of their confidential records."

Tony smiled like a bright and arrogant student and said, "In America we have a word to solve that problem. It's called finesse."

"*Finezze*, we have the same word in Italian. You Americans probably stole it from our language, Mr. Smart Man Morelli. So how will *finezze* help solve the problem of finding where this girl might be enrolled in school?"

Tony dropped his head and thought. After a few moments, he said, "Okay, how about this? I'm thinking out loud, so help me along. I am who I am, Anthony Morelli from America, and you are the future Mrs. Morelli from here in Rome."

Gina raised her eyebrows and added, "And we wish to bring your son or daughter to Rome and live with us."

"Good. Let's make it my son, Jimmy."

"Is he like his father?"

"No, he is ugly and a little dim-witted."

Gina laughed and said, "We wish to enroll him in this international school."

"Yes, but he would be more likely to come to a school where perhaps some of his American friends might be. Could we see the list of American children enrolled here?"

"I am sorry, Mr. Morelli," said Gina taking on the role of a school administrator, "but that is confidential information."

"I understand fully and admire that about your institution. Can I, however, just mention a couple of names of former American schoolmates who I know moved here recently? Let me see, one was Lester Lipshitz and the other . . . what was her name?" Tony thought about what last name Rebecca would use. He remembered the name on the back of her softball uniform. "Ah, yes, Rebecca DiFoggio?"

"*Finezze*. It just might work," Gina said and stood.

They left the boat.

ROME TO HOME

Tommaso picked them up at the Rome airport. He, of course, wanted to know all about the trip. They told him everything—almost everything. Tony harbored a latent fear. He feared that at some tell-all moment, Gina would disclose to Tommaso the intimate moment she and Tony shared at the beach. He was less afraid of the rage of a jealous Italian husband, but more frightened that the respect, the bond and the friendship developed between him and Tommaso would be destroyed.

"So, I conclude that your 'caper', I believe is the English word, now includes research into the international school system here in Rome. I wish I could help, but my knowledge and business connections do not extend into the Italian educational institutions."

Gina turned from the front seat, faced Tony in the back and said, "I, too, must take a break from this caper, as Tommaso calls it. I've already spent too many days beyond the weekend away from my Aunt Pier. She has come to depend on me if only for company. I will only need a few days away from Rome."

"That's fine," said Tony. "I'll need a few days to do some research, reconnect with home and make arrangements for a longer stay."

They dropped him off in front of his hotel and exchanged farewells. Tony stood tall on the sidewalk for a few moments and looked up and down the street. The Eurostars International Palace Hotel, the lame beggar, the bar/café, his own hotel, Nazionale 51—nothing had changed. It seemed as if he had been away for months, not just a few days, and something should be different.

One thing had changed. *No bald guy following me. Was he truly gone? Did our confrontation end the stalking? Was he really stalking me, or did my paranoia force some poor innocent guy to pepper spray me?* He shook his head, picked up his bag and went to his room.

He knew he had things to do: unpack, arrange for a longer stay at the hotel, call Pauline, and research international schools in Rome. When he saw his bed with fresh, white linens and fluffy feathered pillow, he forgot his to-do list and collapsed onto it.

The *All The President's Men* dream had vanished like a ghost from his subconscious. That's the way Tony's mind worked. His subliminal thoughts helped him solve problems. He trusted and respected his subconscious, and he learned to tap into it through dream analysis and self-hypnosis. But after solving a problem, his subconscious took a break. His dreams defaulted into erotic dreams, the majority involving Pauline.

In this dream Pauline sang a blues torch song at Kingston Mines, a Chicago blues nightclub where she often performed and packed the house. Tony stood in the back of the crowd. Pauline sang from a raised stage. She wore only a black lace teddy and moved with seductive bumps and grinds to the hoots and whistles of an all-male audience. Tony fought to get to the front, but every time he tried to squeeze forward, more men appeared in front of him and pushed him toward the door.

He awoke in a cold sweat. It was twilight. He had to call home, but felt he needed a drink and some food first. At the bar/café he drank a couple of gin-and-tonics and ate a plate of assorted antipasto dishes.

He returned to his darkened room. The message light on his phone flashed. He wondered if it had been blinking when he was there earlier but hadn't noticed it in his fatigued state. He hit the message button and listened to Pauline's distraught voice.

"Where have you been? I thought you were going to Sicily for just a day. Call home right away."

Tony dropped the receiver twice before he was able to make the call. There was no answer at his Oak Park apartment, so he tried calling her cell number. Even before he heard her voice, he knew where she was. The discordant sounds of guitar strings, a saxophone and drum rolls told him she was at rehearsal, and her band was warming up.

"Tony?"

"Yeah."

"Where have you been? I've been trying to reach you for two days. I thought you were just going to Sicily for the day, and you didn't answer your cell."

"I thought I'd be back, too, but I ran into a problem tracking this Sagona guy. I left my cell phone in the room to charge. Forget that, are you okay? What's going on? Your message sounded urgent."

The cops are looking for you. Actually, they're looking for Laura DiFoggio, your friend's sister. This Mad Bomber person made a deal with the prosecutor. I don't know the details, but he said she hired him to plant the bomb in your car. She wouldn't tell him why. Like you, they tracked her to the airport, but lost track of her after that. She must have changed her name, identity or something."

"That's what we figured, too."

"We?"

"Gina, Tommaso, her fiancé, and I."

"Well, at least you're not alone. Anyway, they explicitly told me to tell you to call them if you spot her and under no circumstances confront her. She's now listed with the F.B.I. as armed and dangerous. They'll notify the Rome authorities and work out arrest and extradition details."

"And how long will that take? Do they even have anyone here looking for her, other than me?"

"That I don't know, but the bottom line is, be careful."

They talked for a few more minutes before Pauline went back to rehearsal.

Tony wasn't tired anymore. He spent the rest of the night researching the Rome International School Association on his computer. His nocturnal research, in large part a product of cutting and pasting from the internet, produced these notes:

A number of headmasters and principals of schools in Rome founded the Rome International Schools Association in 1974, desiring to share ideas for keeping up to date with the trends of education in their home countries. From those early meetings the Association grew. The schools are of varying sizes and offer different combinations of levels from pre-school through secondary. The schools all share these common factors:

They are "International" in the sense that they offer a curriculum either typical of a country outside Italy or one in which the culture and educational practice of two or more countries are represented.

They have students and sometimes teachers drawn from a number of nations.

Their sole or major language of instruction is English.

14 member schools comprise RISA. Chances are Rebecca DiFoggio would be enrolled in one of the following:

American Overseas School (AOSR) Age Range 3-19

Founded in 1946, AOSR is a day and boarding school located on Rome's north side.

Enthusiastic parents and the United States government invested resources, in order to expand the school grounds and enhance academic facilities. Present enrollment stands at 400 students from the local and international community. Via Cassia, 811 Tel 06 334 381 (Cassia)

Marymount International School-Rome Age Range: 3-18

A private Catholic school, with admission open to students from all nationalities and religious backgrounds, Marymount is known for its highly-praised academic program, extracurricular activities, modern facilities and a strong college preparatory program offering a U.S. secondary school diploma as well as the International Baccalaureate diploma. Via di Villa Lauchli, 180 Tel 06 362 9101 (Vigna Clara/Cassia)

The New School Age Range 3-18

The school follows the English National Curriculum from nursery through secondary school. The Italian Ministry for Education recognizes its educational program and it is an official examination center for Edexcel, and the University of Cambridge International Examinations (CIE). Students can be prepared for the Italian State exams (5a Elementare and 3a Media) and the American SATs..Via della Camilluccia, 669 tel 06 329 4269

St. Stephens School Age Range: 3-19

Founded in 1964 this private day and boarding school offers a rigorous classic liberal arts education, based on preparing children in six major academic areas, following an American curriculum. An easy and relaxed student-teacher relationship promotes learning. Via Aventina, 3 tel 06 575 0605 (Aventina, close to Circus Maximus)

Tony reviewed his notes on the computer screen. *Will these notes lead me to Rebecca, Laura, Todd or Vincenzo? More important, will they lead me to a book or maybe my death?*

The light and morning sounds and smells of trucks delivering bakery goods seeped through his patio door from the street.

He saved his notes to a flash drive and shut down his computer.

TONY TOURIST

He wanted to fall asleep but knew it was a bad idea. Staying up all night had produced artificial jet lag. In other words, his body was conned into thinking the day was the night, without the help of an airplane. Pauline taught him the cure for jet lag. When you arrive at your destination during the day, force yourself to stay awake until night. If you arrive at night, drug yourself to sleep.

It would be two days before Gina would return to Rome, and they could search the international schools for Rebecca. He decided to be a tourist. Sure, he had been to Rome twice before.

The last time was just weeks ago on his book tour, but there had been little time for touring. The first time was years ago when he and Pauline met. Yes, he visited the sights, but he was more focused on Pauline than the wonders of Rome. He grabbed his laminated Rome city map from his folder and a dated Rick Steves' Italy tour book from the hotel lobby and hit the streets.

From the front seat of his Smart car, he opened Rick's book to the chapter on Rome. He skipped over the opening pages. Rick's general advice and travel tips about touring Rome were moot points to Tony. He had already learned by trial and error and could have written his own pamphlet on the dos and don'ts of touring Italy as an American.

Choosing from the hundreds of tempting Roman vistas for a day's sightseeing tour proved challenging. He could cross Victor Emmanuel Monument off his list. His visit there days earlier reminded him too much of his current quest in Italy; his goal this day was to forget his mission. *Can I achieve this goal?*

The section "Rome at a Glance" and Tony's personal favorite tourist attraction choices guided him to highlight four locations on his map: Vatican City, Trevi Fountain, the Roman Forum and the Colosseum.

He decided to start at the place farthest from his hotel, Vatican City. He and Pauline had ditched the Vatican trip from their group tour and opted for a romantic day at the beach, so it was the only attraction on his short list that he hadn't seen before. He wondered if this visit would rekindle the Catholic spirit within him—the spirit a parochial school education forced upon him, cruel nuns beat into him and priests' sermons burned into him. Each year from puberty to adulthood, the spirit dimmed until it flickered out by the end of his college sophomore year and never returned.

His first impression of Vatican City was its vast size. Rick Steves reminded him that Vatican City is "the world's smallest country." His next notion was the irony of a dress code. At St. Peter's Basilica, guards enforced the rules applicable to both men and women: No shorts, skirts or bare shoulders.

It occurred to Tony that if St. Peter, wearing his contemporary tunic and sandals made an appearance, the guards would have turned him away. Tony acknowledged his awe of the ancient intricate architecture and artwork that adorned the interiors of the basilica, illuminated only by natural light and candles.

His artistic appreciation dampened when he opted to climb the narrow, curving stairway to the top of the basilica dome for a panoramic view of Vatican City. The tight unventilated enclosure intensified by streams of tourists ascending and descending the same stairs created a claustrophobic reaction within him.

A traumatic childhood incident had left Tony with a fear of certain enclosed places. A favorite neighborhood before-your-parents-call-you-home-because-it's-getting-too-dark game was hide-and-seek. Most of the hiding places in his residential area were well-known by the kid who was "it," so the game became a matter of "it" searching those places and declaring his or her discovery of the next "it."

Tony discovered a new hideaway at a bungalow that had just burned down. A damaged portion of a floorboard exposed a crawl space beneath the house. Tony squeezed himself under the floor and between the joists and shimmied deep beneath the first level. After sufficient time for "it" to find him, he prepared to crawl backwards and declare himself "free." The tightness made it impossible for him to squirm in the opposite direction. Panic set in. For two and a half hours his screams only echoed within the tiny space and into his ears, which intensified his terror. A woman walking her dog that night reported hearing sounds in the abandoned structure and called police who rescued him.

By the time Tony reached the top of St. Peter's Basilica, he was drenched in sweat and hyperventilating.

He took the elevator down and made the fifteen-minute walk to the Vatican Museum. The museum consisted of almost 12,000 rooms, so the mobs of tourists spread out and allowed Tony to feel relief from his prior oppressive experience. He viewed the elaborate sixteenth century wall and ceiling paintings in the four Raphael Rooms, the gold dress and body jewelry displayed in Rooms VII and VIII, and a room full of antique confession booths rekindling his childhood days of revealing his sins on Saturdays again.

Maybe it was the after effects of his anxiety attack. Maybe it was his lack of religious spirit, but the priceless Vatican jewels and artifacts neither impressed nor overwhelmed him. As he left Vatican City and walked to his parked Smart car, only one thought prevailed. *How can it be Christian to hoard all those expensive things, when more than half the world was starving?*

The Smart car weaved through traffic and over the Tiber River toward Plaza di Spagna. Tony found a parking spot so tight he had to back the vehicle up, so that both rear tires touched the curb and he could look out the narrow windshield and see traffic zoom by. The Spanish Steps were not on his list, but he took a moment to see what Rick Steves had written about them.

"The British poet John Keats pondered his mortality, then died of tuberculosis at age 25 in the pink building on the right side of the steps."

Tony walked to the sight but wasn't interested in seeing the hundreds of tourists climbing, sitting and taking pictures of the 135 stairs. He focused on the pink building and thought about his own mortality. *That car bomb could have killed me. I could get killed here.*

He spun around and expected to see someone, maybe the bald guy, ignoring the crowd and staring at, maybe through him, and holding a gun.

No one was there.

The short walk to Trevi fountain allowed him to relax and to settle his nerves. The warm afternoon sun took its toll, so by the time he reached the fountain he was ready to dive into the cool, clear pool of spouting water. Every kind of tourist, kids-lovers-drunkards, jammed near the water's edge, many engaging in the ritual of tossing coins into it. Tony took advantage of Rick's tip of " . . . a peaceful zone on the far right" and had a cold beer and a prosciutto panini at an outdoor café.

His vantage point, far enough away yet close enough to the crowd, presented an opportunity to scan the multitude for the bald guy—nowhere in sight, but he did make one observation—the difference between American and Italian middle-aged men.

Most middle-aged American men, excluding me, seem to have given up on their appearance. They parade their beer guts with pride over their loose-fitting slacks or walking shorts and let their cheap button-down sport shirts and belly work together and produce shade over their laced-up tennis shoes and white socks. A faded baseball cap with a white/yellow sweat stain where the cap and brim meet the forehead completes the outfit.

Italian middle-aged males and even many seniors dress in a way that says, "I'm still a player." Just like men half their age, their wardrobe includes tapered, tailored designer jeans over trim waistlines, white or bright long-sleeved dress shirts with sleeves folded up the forearm and sandals or dress shoes sans socks.

Following his beer, panini and fashion critique, he drove his car back to the hotel, parked it and took the fifteen minute walk to the area of the Roman Forum and the Colosseum. The

Forum brought Tony a sense of peace. It symbolized order and civilization even during turbulent and unsure ancient times. The setting of this historic place calmed him. Unlike the polished, pristine pavements and buildings in Vatican City, the ruins were set in dust, dirt, and stones of natural earth, almost as if the crumpling pillars and structures had grown up from the soil. It reminded him of the empty lots in Chicago where he had played as a kid. *But what did it mean, that this symbol of a civil society was crumbling into ruins?*

He shook off the thought and crossed the street toward the Colosseum.

"Now I feel like I'm going to a Chicago Bears game at Soldier Field," he said to himself. He marveled at how the modern sports stadiums mimicked this 2,000-year-old arena. He could imagine lights on top, a press box, and vendors selling beer and hot dogs.

The interior reminded him that he wasn't at a football game in Chicago, a soccer game in Brazil, a bullfight in Spain or even a military parade in Nazi Germany. This arena was where humans and vicious animals slaughtered other humans. He looked down at the open underground area where caged lions and gladiators waited to go upstairs to please the blood-thirsty crowd.

He felt himself thinking about his own mortality again. A sweaty tightness overcame him like when he was in the enclosed staircase in the dome. He sat down on a stone and closed his eyes. He could hear the crowd roaring, flesh tearing, and humans screaming. *What's happening to me? Am I having a breakdown?*

His eyes opened.

The screaming stopped.

A class of children and their teacher stared at him.

"*Stai bene?*" asked the teacher.

"I'm fine."

He returned to his hotel, climbed into bed and slept for thirty-six hours.

PLAN B

Nothing woke him. He woke himself up with renewed energy. It was already mid-morning and Rome echoed its bustling vibrations from the street and up to his room. His watch read 9:37 a.m. That didn't surprise him. The date indicated that it was Thursday.

"I slept over thirty hours?" he asked his mirror image over the dresser.

His image returned a confused look, which turned into a smile, a laugh and then a refreshed healthy glow. He couldn't explain it, but he felt great. Whatever conditions had driven him to a near breakdown, hours of deep sleep washed them away and left him rejuvenated.

Gina was due back in Rome this day from her aunt's house in Frosinone. He called her cell number.

"*Pronto?*" Her voice sounded distant and the reception weak.

"It's Tony. Where are you?"

"I'm on a train coming back to Rome. I can barely hear you."

"When's your train due in?"

"In about fifteen minutes."

"I'll pick you up at the station. We've got work to do."

Their connection got cut short. He grabbed his folder and raced down the stairs; the elevator wasted time.

His Smart car circled the parkway outside the station entrance with the big white letters ROMA TERMINI, and he watched for Gina. He saw her looking over the pedestrian rail in the taxi area. He cut in front of the line of taxis and beeped his horn. Almost on cue, the drivers hit their horns and yelled obscenities at him.

Gina hopped inside his Smart car with her travel bag and said, "What are you doing? You are not allowed in the taxi area."

"I could give a shit," he said with an air of confidence.

She laughed and then stared at him as if she wanted to ask something but couldn't find the words. "Did you sleep in those clothes?"

He touched his chin and felt his two-day old beard. "Oh my God, I haven't shaved or showered since Tuesday."

She just smiled, shook her head and said, "Stop up here. We will get some cappuccinos, and you can tell me all about it."

At the outdoor bar/café, Tony recapped the events starting with his all night research and ending with his collapse after a full day of touring.

"You overworked your mind and body. Maybe you need more rest."

"Oh, no. Those thirty some hours of sleep did the trick. I feel like a million bucks."

"You look like old crumpled Italian liras before we started using euros."

Tony choked a little on his cappuccino when he chuckled at her joke. "I'll go back to my hotel and freshen up after this, but let me show you what I came up with." He pulled out the printouts of his notes. He had highlighted the information of four of the fourteen schools and numbered them, one through four. "This is Plan A. First, we visit these schools in this order."

"Why these schools in that order?"

"All I know about Laura's daughter is that she's fourteen, plays softball, and probably doesn't want to be here or at least would rather be with her friends in America. Laura made some remark to her about coming right home after her softball game and not hanging around with boys, so I take it she's starting to get interested in them. With that I eliminated the schools that only went up to what we call middle school or junior high.

"That left these four international schools. As far as the order, I just took a guess. I figured she'd prefer a co-ed school with plenty of athletic choices, but who knows? Laura may have different priorities for her. Also, some are boarding schools. We don't know where they live, so we don't know if boarding school is an option. If she commutes, which I hope, we can follow her home. My guess is that she lives with her mom."

"We talked about our play-acting when we go to these schools. Let us go over it again. What is our story, and what do we say?"

Their cappuccinos arrived. They stirred the surface cream with their little spoons. Tony savored the frothy espresso taste before continuing.

"The less we lie the easier it will be to remember our roles and lines, so we'll keep our real names and occupations. The play-acting, as you call it, will be that we are engaged. I have a son, Jimmy, in the United States. We want to bring him over here to live with us before we get married in October.

"Like most teens in America or maybe anywhere, he has developed friendships and ties at his school and really doesn't want to leave the U.S. He says a girl he knows from his school came to live here in Rome with her mother and enrolled in school, but he doesn't know where. We're sure the odds of her being at this very school are slim. We'll not push it yet, just see if the administrator offers information. If not, we'll inquire about the school its facilities, programs, yadda, yadda, yadda, and seem more and more impressed.

"We'll appear sold on the place, until either you or I think of little Jimmy's feelings. If he knew that, what was her name? Roberta? No, Rebecca was here. That would clinch his decision to come here."

"It sounds like a good plan, and it might even be fun. Now, let us assume that we discover that the girl is registered at the school. What is next?"

"Well, our main goal is to find Laura. We'll ask if we can speak to the mother to get her feelings about the school and why she chose it for her daughter."

"That is where I see a confidentiality problem, maybe."

"Yeah, I thought of that, too. We'll have to come up with a way to find and to follow Rebecca. We may even have to approach her."

Gina sipped her cappuccino and watched pedestrians. She squinted and appeared deep in thought.

"Is something wrong?" asked Tony.

She faced him and replaced her cup to the saucer. "Tony, I am not what one would call a negative person. I think your plan is a good one, but you called it Plan A. What is Plan B?"

He took a long drink from his cappuccino and said, "There is no Plan B."

They spent the morning people watching.

JIMMY-BOY

Tony was ready to start the search that afternoon, but Gina talked him out of it.

"We will start fresh tomorrow morning. You are in Italy now, not America."

He had learned what she meant. Italians worked on a different time schedule than Americans. As a matter of fact, most of Europe, in particular the warmer regions, lived by that timetable. It's rooted in the days when Europe was more of an agrarian continent. People awoke at dawn and worked hard until noon. After lunch, they slept during the sultry afternoon. At dusk, some returned to the fields while others partied through the night.

The trend continued into modern times. Many businesses close for lunch and reopen in the evening, even during tourist season. Tony's uncle who spent his childhood in Sicily kidded about the Italian work schedule. "If you listen closely at noon, you can hear all of Italy say at the same time, 'Fuck it. I'm taking a nap'."

Gina contacted each of the four schools that afternoon for appointments the following day.

Friday morning, Tony picked up Gina at her and Tommaso's condo, and they began their engaged couple act.

He chose The New School for their first visit. He based his choice mainly from his imagining in which school he might enroll a daughter or son with Rebecca's characteristics. The institution bragged of a rich academic curriculum that prepared students to take college entrance exams in America including the SAT. This might speak to Rebecca's dream of returning home to the U.S.

It also had a reputation for providing a variety of athletic programs. Another basis for his choice was wishful thinking. The New School was not a boarding school. If Rebecca commuted to and from school, it might be easier to follow her home and to locate her mother.

The New School was set in a residential area on the north side of Rome, not far from historic Piazza del Popolo. The central building appeared to have been a former two-story mansion. Several other smaller buildings, with shaded paved pathways connecting them, spread out behind the mansion among leafy fruit trees.

They arrived fifteen minutes early for their 8:00 a.m. appointment and took the opportunity to stroll the grounds. Beyond the smaller units, a playground, soccer field, track and flat grassy field opened to about an acre of land.

As they made their way back to the main building, several adults carrying cardboard boxes, posters and plastic bags entered the classroom buildings using their own keys. A tall, thin, smiling middle-aged woman met them at the rear door of the mansion, extended a hand and said, "Mr. Morelli and Ms. Sagona?"

"Yes," they answered in unison.

"I am Carlotta Burnetti, Head Teacher and Chairman of the Executive Council of The New School," she said with a crisp British accent. "I hope you don't mind that I used your English honorifics, Mr. and Ms., we try to speak strictly English here."

"Not at all," said Gina.

"As you may have noticed, some of our teachers are preparing their classrooms for the coming term which starts in a few weeks. We do have orientation and remedial programs during the summer for new students wanting to get a running start into the term, and struggling students needing extra help, but those classes don't begin for another hour."

Tony wondered if they might spot Rebecca at an orientation class.

"Follow me inside, please."

If the outside could be mistaken for a residential dwelling, the inside looked like the administrative center of a school district in a typical small town in America. Two reception desks faced the front entrance, and a waiting area between the desks and the front door with several straight-backed chairs and a magazine rack greeted visitors. A young man dressed in a suit and holding a file folder sat in one of the chairs. One receptionist filled a file cabinet with folders and the other ran off copies of a booklet on a copy machine.

Tony and Gina followed the head teacher to the front, where she held open a door next to the waiting room and invited them inside. Her office was the same size as the entire waiting room, reception area and office machine section. It was really an office/board room/kitchen. She asked them to sit at the long table. Two brochures and bound booklets had already been placed at their assigned places. Ms. Burnetti sat at the head of the table.

"So, Ms. Sagona tells me you are engaged to be married. You, Mr. Moretti, wish to bring your son here to Italy, and you are considering enrolling him in The New School."

"That's correct," said Tony, and Gina nodded.

"Our normal procedure is for me to tell parents what The New School offers. Later, you can tell me about your son, and together we can decide if The New School is a correct fit for him."

She went through the entire booklet, page by page, with them. It included a brief history of the school, the curriculum, the extra-curricular activities, and statistics about enrollment and test scores. Every page included at least one photo of students engaged in a classroom activity, playing on an athletic field or enjoying a field trip. The final pages of the packet contained a tear-out section with application forms and registration requirements.

"Of course, you would want to know what the costs are for attending here," she said and handed them a separate sheet.

They both acted as if the figures were quite reasonable, but later shared their shock at the fees. It would cost approximately 18,000 euros a year for their son to attend The New School, not including registration and book fees.

"Are you still interested in enrolling your son here?" she asked.

Gina looked at Tony as if the decision were all his.

"Yes, very much so," he said.

"Well, it would have been beneficial if your son could be here now, but let us discuss him and see if he might feel comfortable here. What is his name? How old is he, and what are his academic and extra-curricular interests?"

"Jimmy-Boy. We all call him Jimmy-Boy, but his full name is James Morelli. I hate to brag, but he's what we Americans call a chip-off-the-old-block, a lot like his dad. He's bright, especially in math and literature and quite an athlete."

Gina opened her pamphlet, bit her lip and hid her smile that threatened to evolve into a laugh.

"Loves soccer, baseball and basketball."

"He sounds like an interesting young man. What about his social skills?"

Tony looked as if he were somewhat at a loss for words.

"Is there a problem, Mr. Morelli? I mean does Jimmy-Boy, James, have trouble in that area?"

"Oh, no, Ms. Burnetti, Jimmy-Boy has many friends. That's the problem. He gets along well with people. The problem is, excited as he may be to live with us here in Rome, he is sad and reluctant to leave his American friends."

"That is quite normal. Our student population primarily consists of children from the United States and Great Britain. We are familiar with the problem of students feeling homesick. Our excellent counseling staff offers programs and strategies to help students and parents to deal with that problem."

"Great, but . . . I wondered . . . Oh, I suppose the odds would be against it."

"Go ahead and ask, Tony," Gina encouraged him. "What would it hurt?"

"Well," he said, "Tony mentioned a schoolmate of his. Roberta, was it?"

"No, I think he said, 'Rebecca.' Yes, Rebecca."

"Yes, Rebecca or Roberta DiFoggio came to live with her mother here in Rome. She had mentioned that she was supposed to register at an international school, but he didn't know the name. I was wondering if it might be The New School. If that were the case, my inclination would be to get my checkbook out and begin the admission process."

Carlotta stared at him for a few seconds, just enough to create tension.

Is the answer, "No?" Does she suspect we are fakes?

She picked up her phone, pushed a button and said, "Maria, check and see if we have registered a Rebecca DiFoggio for the fall term or summer orientation."

Tony and Gina sighed at the same time. While waiting for the results, they participated in small talk—Rome, the weather, Tony's and Gina's wedding plans.

The receptionist appeared in the doorway and said, "Ms. Burnetti, we do not see that name in the computer files or the stack of registration applications to be entered."

"Thank you, Maria." Carlotta focused back on Tony and Gina. "I hope the answer does not dampen your consideration of The New School."

"Not at all," said Tony.

"We will discuss it tonight with Jimmy-Boy," Gina almost cracked up when she said the name, "and get back to you."

In the car, they couldn't contain their laughter.

"Jimmy-Boy? Chip-off-the-old-block? Where did that come from?"

"Hey, we were quite the acting duo," Tony said and held up his hand for a high-five. He had to educate her on the ritual.

"She slapped his palm and said, "Marlon Brando and Anna Magnani."

"I wish you would have chosen living actors."

*****

They didn't have to drive far to get to American Overseas School of Rome (AOSR). Situated on Rome's north side, they parked in the lot off Via Cassia and surveyed the grounds. The manicured lawn with shaded study areas, trimmed hedges, flower beds, and paved paths crossing through the park and leading to the central building gave it the look of a prestigious private university.

"So tell me," asked Gina. "Why is this our second choice?"

"It's actually my first choice. The New School doesn't provide boarding. I was hoping that would lend itself more to following Rebecca home to her mom. They still may live in this area, but most students pay room and board. She can still lead us to Laura if she lives on campus. It just might be a little more complicated and require more *finezze*."

The central building reminded Tony of his old high school. It was an old, but sturdy three-story structure with a clock tower over the top roof. Every floor had classroom windows, but inside the wide main entrance there were no classrooms, just offices. A hallway, as wide as the front entrance, led to the rear of the building, where another entrance of equal width opened to massive grassy fields.

From just inside the main entrance they could see through the back glass doors. Kids played soccer. Tennis courts, volleyball nets and basketball courts loomed farther away. Smaller classroom buildings and single story dormitories surrounded the recreational area. In the center of the spacious hallway a sign with a white-painted arrow pointing left read: ALL VISITORS MUST GO DIRECTLY TO THE MAIN OFFICE.

A receptionist in the glassed-in main office directed them across the hall to a smaller office labeled ADMISSIONS. Two sentences into Tony's spiel about their quest to register Jimmy-Boy, the secretary interrupted. "We would like you to view our orientation video," she said and led them to a room with cushioned chairs and a giant television screen. "I'll return in about ten minutes and turn on the lights."

The teachers, parents, and students narrated the presentation, which was a virtual tour of the school . The viewer visited classrooms at all levels and saw snippets of athletic competition and learning situations. Most of the teachers were Americans, and the production left one thinking that he or she had just visited a K through 12 public school in the U.S.

The secretary returned and brought them to the Head of Admissions office of Dr. Sally Newman. To Tony, the attractive administrator looked like a taller, older version of Gina. She was very polite but appeared to be very busy with other work.

"Do you have any questions regarding the orientation video?" she asked. Without waiting long for a response, she handed them a packet similar in content to The New School booklet. "Why don't you both peruse these materials for a few minutes while I finish some work here and then we can talk?"

They skimmed through the papers and pretended to be awed. Tony waited until the administrator appeared to be finished with her work, and then wasted no time getting to the point. "Dr. Newman, I think I speak for both myself and my fiancé when I say that we are quite impressed with this institution and would be eager to enroll my son here. My, well our, son Jimmy pleaded with us to ask just one important question—"

"Tony, dear, the chance of her being here is very small," Gina interrupted.

"I know, but if she were here he'd beg us to come here, and I'd almost be willing to write a check right now."

"Please, Mr. Morelli, what would you like to know?"

"He asked us to find out if his former schoolmate from America had enrolled, yet . . ."

As soon as he had pronounced her full name, the woman said, "Becky?"

They both sat up straight as if Dr. Newman was a teacher calling on them to recite.

"Yes," they responded.

"Becky has already enrolled in our four-day-per-week summer orientation session. It's more like a summer camp with both academics and recreation. She boards here, but I'm afraid you missed her. After the last weekly session ended yesterday, she and most of the others spend the weekend with family.

"It's too bad that you missed her. I'm sure she'd be happy to know that a former schoolmate might be coming here. She is doing much better now, but I'm afraid she still feels a little homesick as many of our students do for the first few months. Oh, and I am also sorry to say that it's a little too late for your son to attend the summer session. Next week is our last week. Two and a half weeks after that, we start our regular school year."

Neither Gina nor Tony tried to hide their elation.

"By your reactions, it looks as if your son would also be happy to see Becky and hopefully be a fellow student."

"Definitely."

"He'll be speechless."

They had almost forgotten their roles.

"One more thing, Dr. Newman. Would you mind if we contacted her mother or father to get a reference for the school?"

Dr. Newman gave Tony a sympathetic smile and said, "I have no problem with you seeking a reference; however, contact information concerning our students is confidential. I can tell you that her parents are listed as deceased. Her uncle is her legal guardian."

Tony and Gina gasped in unison.

FLORENCE

"Now what?"

"Good question," said Tony.

They sat in the Smart car and stared at the black hands of the huge clock on the tower pointing toward the sky from the top of the American Overseas School of Rome building. It was close to noon, and their mission to find Rebecca or Becky was over.

"But two things are certain," he added. "We can't do anything until Monday."

"True."

"And we have to wrap this thing up, answer all our questions about Laura, Todd and Vincenzo by the end of the week."

"Why is that?"

"I'm running out of money and plans."

They sat in silence and watched two white gulls peck at the grass on the school lawn.

"If you have no plans for the weekend, you can spend some time with me and Tommaso."

"No, I do have plans," he said as if he had rehearsed his answer. "I'm driving to Florence."

"Florence? Why?"

"I have three goals before I leave Italy. First, I need to buy Pauline an anniversary gift. She gave me a beautiful car, and I thanked her by getting it, and almost her, blown up. I should have gotten it when I was in Florence on the Ponte Vecchio during my book tour, but I didn't."

"May I guess what it will be?"

"No, it's a secret, even to myself."

"And your other two missions?"

"I have to see if I'm still being followed. I haven't seen that bald guy or noticed anyone else since I had my little altercation with him. Somehow I still feel like I'm being watched. I don't know, maybe I'm just being paranoid. My last mission is to come up with an answer to your 'Now what?' question."

He dropped off Gina at Tommaso's condo where they exchanged farewell hugs and European pecks on each cheek.

At his hotel, he asked the padrone for recommendations of hotels near the Ponte Vecchio, the famous exclusive Italian jewelry area located on the historic bridge over the Arno River in Florence. The hotel owner made reservations for him for Saturday night at Hotel Torre Guelfa Palazzo. Tony hoped it would be easier to find than to pronounce.

*****

He woke up Saturday morning and took the three-hour drive northwest on highway A/1 to Florence. During the entire ride, his eyes peeked at his rearview mirror every few minutes. Each time that he was convinced the car behind him was following, the vehicle sped past his Smart car on the left and disappeared.

It was too early to check into his hotel when he arrived around noon, so he parked in a private lot near the hotel, had an antipasto lunch and a beer at a restaurant, and walked to Ponte Vecchio. From a distance, the bridge looked like a three-story strip mall of medieval buildings built across a river. Tony knew little about the history of Ponte Vecchio, except that it was the only bridge in Florence the Germans didn't destroy in WWII and that the term 'bankruptcy,' may have originated there.

The legend dating back to the seventeenth century held that when an entrepreneur couldn't pay his rent, the *polizia* destroyed, *rotto*, his table of merchandise, his *banco*. The act became known as *bancorotto* or broken table probably from the term *banca rotta* or broken bank. He mused at the irony. *Here I am with little cash and a credit card at the richest bridge in the world, where the word bankruptcy originated, and I'm here to buy an expensive gift.*

Each little store housed as much as millions of euros worth of bracelets, necklaces, rings, charms, jeweled gifts and earrings. The merchants kept the doors locked and only allowed one or two customers inside at a time. Tourists jammed the bridge, closed to all motor vehicles. Pedestrian traffic moved at the pace of a funeral in both directions, while vacationers marveled at the expensive gifts and jewelry at each tiny shop and moved on to the next.

Tony joined the hordes of window shoppers. Unlike most of them, he entered many of the shops to inquire about the cost and value of items that attracted him. A gold music box captivated him. Rubies symbolic of Pauline's hair surrounded a star sapphire, reminiscent of her blue eyes, on the lid. A card indicated that opening the lid tripped a musical rendition of "Volare." He bought the music box and shopped for another hour.

After buying his last item, he looked at his watch. He had spent the entire afternoon on the bridge. Tired from driving all morning and shopping all afternoon in the hot sun with the swarms of tourists, Tony checked into his hotel. He ate a big pasta dinner at a restaurant within an outdoor plaza around the corner of his hotel—called Trattoria dei Quattro Leoni—and settled into his room with a bottle of Nero D'Avola, and the English version of CNN on the television.

When he woke up, CNN was still blaring, his bottle of wine was near empty and the sunlight filtered through his thin drapes, brightening the room. He turned off the TV and ordered room service breakfast.

On the balcony terrace outside his room, he finished his cappuccino and watched the morning rays make the Florence Duomo in the distance look gold. He contemplated his goals for the weekend.

I definitely accomplished the goal of buying Pauline's gift. I hope she'll be surprised. Did I solve the mystery about being followed? There is no evidence of anyone stalking me anymore, so I have to assume no one was or is tracking me . . . but I still feel shadowed. Now, the big question: How should Gina and I handle our encounter with Rebecca tomorrow and uncover the truth about her mother and uncles? Should we just follow her? Confront her? I have some ideas. Maybe they'll come to fruition before Monday.

Whether it was his appreciation of art, respect for world history or a deep-seated Catholic education, Tony knew he couldn't leave Florence without viewing Michelangelo's David. He had seen it once before on his first trip to Italy, but the iconic statue begged repeated viewing. He checked the Rick Steves' guidebook he had "borrowed" from his Rome hotel. The Accademia Museum stayed open all day Sunday.

He packed his bag and checked out of his hotel. His plan was to visit the museum and then return to Rome. It was lucky that he had checked out first. During tourist season, without a reservation, which Tony lacked, one stood in line for hours; he would have had to pay for another night. For Tony, it was worth the three-hour wait.

The statue overwhelmed Tony the same way it had the first time he saw it. As a kid, the David and Goliath story had mesmerized him. His Catholic education can't take credit for revealing the biblical story to him. It was Coach Kelley, Tony's junior football league coach, who inspired his aspiring young athletes with the tale.

"Young men, our battle today reminds me of the true story of the Israelites facing the Philistines. The Philistines were giants. Every day for forty days, their giant of the giants, an eight-foot guy named Goliath, stood before the Israelites and said, 'If just one of you Jews has the balls to kick my ass, you win this battle, and you can keep your land. No one challenged him for those forty days. Then, this skinny kid named David, the Israelite's towel boy, said, 'I'm tired of this pussy-ass shit. If you old farts won't fight this guy, I will.'

"When the elders couldn't talk him out of it, they tried to give him weapons, but David refused. He stripped down to his bare-assed naked self and faced the giant. Goliath, dressed in full armor, looked at the kid and just laughed. But while he was laughing, the little towel boy noticed something. Goliath's helmet was too small and didn't cover his forehead. He picked up a stone and borrowed a slingshot from one of his fellow towel boys. With one shot, he hit Goliath square in the noggin and killed him. Then, David cut off his head, and the Jews played football with it the rest of the day. Boys, today our opponent is Goliath and we . . ."

As expected, Tony's team got slaughtered 56-0, but the inspiring story stuck with him. It often stood as a metaphor in his life. The seventeen-foot sculpture symbolized things Tony valued in life: strength, not brute strength, but power backed by civilized, rational thought and courage; youthful spirit; optimism. *Do I have the strength, vigor and positivity to uncover the truth about Laura, Todd and Vincenzo without getting myself, or someone else killed?*

His philosophical thoughts turned to more earthly observations. Michelangelo endowed David with an oversized right hand. He recalled the junior high schoolyard myth or science question: *Does the length of one's fingers predict how long his penis will be?* He glanced at the statue's genitals. David didn't seem to support the mythic argument. Tony looked at his own hands.

It was time to go back to Rome.

BECKY

On Monday at 7:28 a.m., Gina and Tony sat in the Smart car parked in the American Overseas School of Rome lot. They sipped from paper cups of *Il McCafe*. Yes, McDonald's had come to Rome.

No other vehicles had arrived.

"So, review your master plan again for me," said Gina.

"You woke me up, not Tommaso. He is a noisy, sound sleeper. I only half understood what you said except you were picking me up at seven, and we were coming here."

"I went online to the AOSR website as soon as I got home from Florence. Their summer session or camp as this Dr. Newman called it begins at 8 o'clock. I only saw Rebecca or Becky one other time, so I'm hoping I can recognize her. If her mother drops her off, we'll follow her.

"You can call the police and tell them why she needs to be arrested while I drive. Somewhere down the line of police interrogations, we'll have to know the truth about her, Todd and Vincenzo. That's the essence of my next book and hopefully the end of Laura and her attempts on my life, not to mention revenge for what she almost did to Pauline."

"What if her uncle, whoever he turns out to be, brings her?"

"Then, we follow him and hope he leads us to her. I'm fairly confident she isn't 'deceased' like it appears on the school records. Faking one's death and assuming another's identity is a good way to stay hidden, especially in a foreign country. If he doesn't lead us to Laura, we can see if the authorities will question him about the whereabouts of his fugitive sister."

"Let me present one more possible event, other than she does not arrive at all. What if she gets here by taxi or some form of public transportation?"

"*Finezze.*"

"Excuse me?"

"We have to use finesse. I don't know if she'd remember me. I don't know if she's been told anything about me. But if she's been told I'm bad or that she should avoid talking to me, she may run, cause a scene or even have me arrested like her uncle threatened. Somehow, I have to gain her trust. I want you to go to the front desk and tell them you wish to speak to her."

"Who should I say I am?"

"The same person you were on Friday. Tell them you talked to Dr. Newman, and she thought it would be helpful for Becky to know that someone she knew from the U.S. was enrolling at the school. When she comes to the office, tell her that the person, a former schoolmate and softball player, wants to surprise her outside on the front lawn."

"When she comes out, I'll be hiding behind that big tree. That's when I'll confront her."

"Now, the obvious question, what if she refuses to talk to you, decides to run or have you arrested?"

"I'll say the only thing that will make her want to talk with me, and it may very well be true."

"And what is that?"

"I am her ticket back to America."

The first cars brought staff: office workers, summer teachers and administrators, including Dr. Newman. Their Smart car parked in the far corner drew little if any attention. Between 7:45 and 8:00, cars streamed into the lot in masses. Tony tried to keep up with the drop offs but didn't recognize any of the students or drivers. A shuttle bus stopped in front of them. By the time Tony and Gina exited the car, the mob of children of all ages who had left the bus dispersed either toward the main building or the field and structures behind it.

They waited until about 8:15 to let the front premises clear and to allow the students to settle into their environment before Gina went inside.

"Wish me luck," she said and slammed the car door.

Tony wished more than that. He almost wished he had never noticed Todd or his twin in Palermo earlier that summer.

That encounter, his curious nature, and love of a good story had cost him money, time and—almost—his and Pauline's lives. His life might still be in jeopardy. Now, it all came down to these next few minutes. Either Becky would lead him to Laura and her uncle, or it was all over. There was no Plan B.

As the minutes went by, he thought the worst. Rebecca somehow got wise to their ruse. She not only refused to go with Gina, she had Gina detained or arrested.

He peeked from behind the tree and saw the main door open. Gina and Becky emerged and walked toward the study table beneath the shade of the tree. Her blond hair had been cut short and tinted light brown. If it weren't for her limp, somewhat like Todd's, he never would have recognized her.

Becky seemed to be asking questions, and Gina gave short answers and smiled. With each response, Becky got more excited until they sat down at the table. That's when Tony appeared from behind the tree.

"Hi, Becky. Do you remember me?"

She turned and faced him. Her jaw dropped, and she squinted as if she were trying to recall his face. After a few seconds, her eyes widened. She said, "You're the guy who said you knew my uncle—the guy who came to our house. I'm not supposed to talk to you. What's going on? This is a trick!"

She stood up to leave, but Tony put his hands on her shoulders and said, "Do you want to go back home to your friends in Tinley Park, Becky?"

His words stopped her, but she still stood rigid and ready to run.

"Please, Becky, just hear me out for a minute. Afterwards, you can go back inside and never have to see me again, but if you don't listen, I promise, you'll never be able to go back to the United States again."

He removed his hands from her shoulders and stepped back.

Her look remained the same, but she seemed to be focused somewhere into space. She closed her eyes and sighed.

"Okay, I'll listen," she said and sat on the bench.

TRUTH OR CONSEQUENCES?

A black and white cat scurried up the tree. Tony watched it for a moment as it went higher and higher up the leafy branches before he spoke.

"Becky, I don't know what you know about me or anything else. I can only tell you the truth. My name is Tony Morelli, and I'm a writer. Yes, I knew your Uncle Todd from when we were kids, specifically from Little League, but I lost touch when he, your mother and grandparents moved to Flossmoor.

"I hadn't thought much about him over the years, but just last month I thought I saw him in Sicily when I was on a book tour. When I confronted him, well, let's just say he didn't want to see me. Curiosity led me to discover that he had killed himself here in Rome."

Becky looked down at the table, but didn't respond.

"Anyway, as a writer, I thought I might research all this for a possible story. I interviewed your grandmother, and came to your house for the same reason. Your mom was very cordial until I told her my intent to investigate and to write a story about your uncle. She practically threw me out.

"Not long after that a . . . well, let's just say that something terrible almost happened to me. The police seem to feel that maybe your mom or uncle had something to do with it. That's when you left the country. Becky, did you know any of this?"

She continued to stare at the table as if she were in a trance.

Her eyes welled and she said, "I really want to go back home, but they told me if I said anything I'll never go home."

"Who are they?" asked Gina.

"I can't tell you. I don't know who to believe anymore."

Gina put her arms around Becky as she sobbed. "Becky, the man that is your uncle, whoever he is, he is also my first cousin."

Becky lifted her head and looked into Gina's eyes.

"Yes, Becky, we are all related."

"Look, Becky, I only need to know two things. Where is your mother, and who is your uncle? Once I have those answers, I can start arranging for you to go back home," said Tony.

She looked intrigued, but not totally convinced.

"Can I think about it until tomorrow?"

"Of course," said Tony. "We'll meet you here tomorrow at the same time."

"Tony," said Gina, "I won't be able to be here. My aunt needs me in Frosinone."

"Is that okay with you, Becky, if it's just me?"

"I guess so," she said, but didn't sound convincing.

Gina hugged her and said, "It will all be okay, dear."

Becky returned to the school.

GOOD-BYE, TONY

Neither Tony nor Gina spoke during the drive to Tommaso's condo. The silence didn't make sense. There should have been some elation or even celebration. After tomorrow, they would either know the truth or not, and that would be the end of it. Maybe that was the reason for the silence—it would be the end of it.

Tony and Gina had formed a unique bond, not quite lovers but closer than just friends. It was the kind of bond soldiers, after they had gone through battles together, had tried to define without much success.

"So, why the silence and long face?" asked Tony as he pulled into the narrow driveway.

"I'm not sure. I have a bad feeling about all this."

"Hey, one way or another we'll have some kind of closure, even if we don't like it, and I'll call you right away."

"No, it's more than that." She grabbed him by the back of his neck and said, "I care about you, Tony Morelli, and I think you might be in grave danger."

He looked out the window and tried to shrug off her concern.

"These people tried to have you killed. Now, they know you are here looking for them and threatening to expose whatever secrets they hide. Take me seriously and be careful." She gave him a long kiss on the lips and left.

After a late lunch, he called Pauline and told her about his meeting the following day with Becky and that he'd be coming home soon.

"Come home now," she said.

"Why? What's wrong?"

"Nothing."

"No, it's something. Tell me."

"It's silly."

"Tell me anyway."

"I. . . I just had a bad dream last night. You know how our dreams work for us. Your dreams help you write and solve problems. Mine seem to be prophetic."

Tony, who didn't believe in clairvoyance, knew what she meant. Whenever she had a dream about her twenty-two year old son who lived in New York, she'd call him. She had dreamed that he had broken his leg. She called him and found out that he had done just that on a skiing trip. Another time, she woke up in the night with just a feeling that he was in trouble. An hour later, the phone rang, and he had been arrested on a drug possession charge.

"Tell me about it."

"We were some place in Italy, maybe Florence at that huge Duomo. We were climbing stairs to get to the top for a view. You were way ahead. Every time I called for you to wait for me, you got farther and farther away. When I reached the top, no one was there, no one. I looked over the rail and crowds of people stood looking at something. I knew it was your body."

"You're right."

"You're coming home now?"

"No, it's silly. You mixed up me being here with Todd Kenilworth's suicide and who-knows-what. What's your schedule for the week?"

"I'm booked at Kingston Mines from Wednesday through Friday and no gigs for the weekend."

"I'll see you before you finish your first set on Thursday."

She seemed to feel better by the end of their conversation.

When he hung up his room phone, he missed the cradle, and the receiver fell to the floor. His hand had been shaking.

THE BLACK AND WHITE CAT

Tony looked everywhere for the black and white cat that had scampered up the tree the day before, as he sat at the table and waited for Becky.

Will she even show up? Walk right past me? Say she decided not to talk to me? Maybe she told her mother, and I'm being set up. Laura tried to have me killed once, and she failed. Why not try again while she had the chance?

The staff and students arrived just as they had the previous day. No one dropped off Becky. She left the bus, walked straight toward Tony and sat across from him.

"My mother wants to meet with you."

"Why? I mean why now? What changed her mind? Am I being set up for something?"

Becky looked confused. "I don't what you mean by 'set up for something.' We had a big fight last night. I accused her of lying to me about ever going home. She told me I was too young to know everything now. When I threatened to run away whenever I got the chance, she broke down and cried.

"She said she only wanted the best for me and for me to be happy. She told me to tell you she's willing to 'come clean,' whatever that means, and tell you the whole truth, so I can go back home to America—but only under certain conditions."

"What conditions?"

"She chooses the time and place."

"Fine, but no dark alleys or secluded places. I want it to be in a public place where I can feel safe."

"If she thinks she or you are being followed or there are any police around, she won't show up. Just the three of us, and she'll tell us both everything."

"That's fair."

"Do you know where Piazza Venezia is?"

"I'll find it."

"Across the street is a big statue called the Altar of the Fatherland. It's a public place with a lot of tourists. Meet me there today at 5:30, and I'll take you to see my mom." Becky stood up. After she said, "See you then," she did something Tony had never seen her do; she smiled.

As she walked toward the building, he believed that she in fact trusted her mother, and she felt she'd be returning home soon.

A branch shook above him.

The black and white cat had been there the whole time.

THE ALTAR OF THE FATHERLAND

When Tony checked his laminated city map of Rome, he could have kicked himself. The other name for the Altar of the Fatherland is the Victor Emmanuel Monument, the place where Todd Kenilworth was alleged to have killed himself.

As he crossed the busy street between Piazza Venezia and the monument steps, a soothing calm overtook him. The place crawled with tourists. Behind and far above the statue, people crowded to the railing of the observation deck to see and to photograph panoramic views of many of the sites of historic Rome. Not only would he be safe here, it made sense to him that Laura would want to "come clean" at this place. She could explain in exact terms what happened that led to the tragedy here.

Tony was early, but Becky already stood at the top of the steps and waved at him.

"Becky, I hardly know you, but somehow I get the feeling you're feeling happier now than before. Why is that?"

"I'm going home," she said and couldn't hold back a laugh accompanied with the formation of a few tears. "Well, that is if everything works out right today. Mom is watching us somewhere up there." She pointed toward the observation deck. "If she thinks there are no police, you're not being followed, and you're not pulling any tricks, she'll explain everything about her and my uncle . . . to both of us. You're not trying to fool her, are you Mr. Morelli?"

"Absolutely not. I want this thing over with, too, Becky, so I can go home."

She surprised Tony, and maybe herself, when she gave him a warm hug and then took his hand as they walked behind the statue and toward the elevator.

It cost seven euros to ride the glassed-in elevator to the top of the observation deck. Becky reached inside her purse, but Tony insisted on paying for both of them. While waiting in the short line for the elevator to descend and unload, Tony began reading the information about the observation deck.

It stayed open twenty-four hours, but the elevator closed at 5:45 p.m., and visitors would then have to use the stairwells at both ends of the monument. The signs at the entrances to the steps read: CLIMB AT YOUR OWN RISK in four languages. As the elevator rose to the top, he glanced at his watch; it was already 5:35. His heart beat faster with every meter the elevator ascended.

Would she be there? Will I finally learn the truth? Am I being set up like I had originally thought?

The elevator doors opened, and Becky ran to the middle of the deck. She scanned the surroundings with a pensive look on her face. Tony walked toward her just as she focused on the far end of the deck, held her hands up high and said, "Mom, we're over here."

Tony joined Becky and looked in that same direction.

Laura stood at the railing. She smiled and looked relieved. When Tony and Becky walked toward her, she held up her hand and indicated that she'd come to them.

"Hello, Laura. It's good to see you again," Tony said and extended his hand.

She ignored him, grasped Becky's arm and pulled her toward the elevator.

"What are you doing? What's going on?" asked Becky.

"Come on, before the elevator closes. I'll explain on the way down."

"Wait, Laura. There's no one with me. I didn't bring po—"

He felt something poke into his spine. A low male voice said, "The barrel of a Berretta M9 is sticking directly in your back through my sport coat pocket. Follow my directions and everything will work out fine."

The elevator doors closed on an angry, confused girl and her fast-talking mother.

POOR VINCENZO

"Walk slowly toward the railing at the far end. Get a good view of the Colosseum and remember, I'm right behind you with my Beretta pointed at you."

Tony followed the instructions, leaned onto the rail, turned and faced the man. It was the same guy who had clipped him on the jaw in Palermo.

"Sorry I had to tag you so hard in Sicily, but I couldn't let you identify me."

"You got me good, Todd. Never saw it coming. Just like I could never hit your fastball."

Todd chuckled to himself and said, "Ah, Little League. Those were the days. Weren't they, Tony? The age of innocence."

"What happened to that 'innocence,' Todd? I mean it is good to see you here and not down there where the press said you'd jumped to your death. I guess that was your twin brother, Vincenzo."

"Poor Vincenzo. We needed a sacrificial lamb. I guess you might as well know the whole truth since we're almost at the end."

Tony felt his palms sweat when Todd said, ". . . the end."

A voice from a loudspeaker announced that the elevator was now closed and that people would have to use the stairwells at each end to get down.

"Where did it all start, Todd? When you and Terry DiFoggio stole all that money from the mob after that Chicago train construction project fell through?"

"You're pretty smart, Tony—too smart. Maybe it started there. No, that was the good part. I held the money in a private trust overseas for both of us. No one knew about it, not the mob, the IRS, no one. Even when Terry died his tragic death during 9/11, the money would still be there for me, Laura and little Becky. Then, that pain-in-the-ass Chicago Tribune reporter decided to do that where-are-they-now story about surviving Chicago relatives of 9/11 victims. The mob and the IRS were all over my ass. I knew that my real mother lived not far from Rome, so we took a trip here just to let things cool off and see if she, unknowingly, could let me hide out here until I could figure out what to do. That's when I learned I had an identical twin."

"Poor Vincenzo."

"That's right. Poor feeble-minded Vincenzo."

The crowd on the observation deck had thinned out. A worker placed signs in front of the brown wooden doors leading to the staircases at each end of the deck. One read: *INGRESSO VIETATO*, DO NOT ENTER and the other: *USCITA*, EXIT.

"That gave me a perfect plan."

Tony felt anxious. "So, let me guess. You find him, dress him up like you, give him your identification, lure him up here and somehow push him over or get him to jump."

"Close, Tony, close. Laura was against the whole thing, but when I told her it was either him or me and if it was me, she'd never get a cent, our sibling love blossomed and our morals disintegrated. We convinced him that when all the tourists were gone, Laura wanted to take a picture of the two of us on the edge of the deck from down below. I, also, chose this monument as kind of a sick private joke. You know the Romans call that statue down there the ridiculous cake. Well, Vincenzo and I shared the same birthday. Why not add a little humor to all this?"

"You're a real funny guy, Todd."

"When we stepped over the railing, I pushed him over the side."

"Is that the plan you have for me, Todd?"

Todd didn't answer. He just stared at Tony.

"Tony, Tony, why did you have to be so nosey? After I found out you were on to me from Laura, and my mother mentioned you, I panicked. I didn't want to, but I had Laura contact Nicky Altobelli, former client of mine, a psycho known as the Mad Bomber. When my car bombing idea failed, you should have just backed off. I wouldn't risk another attempt. Now I have no choice."

The last two people went down the stairway by the *USCITA* sign.

"Sure you do. Just let me walk away. I'll forget the whole thing and go home. Besides, what chance have you got to get away with it twice? How do you know someone won't come up here by one of those staircases?"

"Didn't you think I'd do my homework, Tony? This place is perfect after the elevator closes. No one is allowed to use the exit stairs to come up here. The entrance stairwell is so hot by this time of day, that even the majority of people who take the challenge of walking the many steps, give up before they're halfway here.

"After I pushed poor Vincenzo over the ledge, I had plenty of time to put on my costume hidden in the down staircase. No one used those stairs to run up here or see if someone was coming down. If they had, all they would have seen was a tired old man with a limp hobbling down the steps."

Tony was terrified. Todd was too far away for him to make a desperate leap for his pocketed gun. All he could do was obey and hope an idea or a miracle would save him.

"Step over the railing and walk to the edge."

He followed Todd's orders.

"Don't worry, my childhood buddy, I'm right behind you. I promise you won't feel a thing."

Three sounds: the shuffle of cloth as Todd pulled something from his pocket, a popping sound and the thud of a body hitting concrete below.

DÉJÀ VU

Tony's arms wrapped around the concrete white washed leaf structure that protruded over the ledge. He peeked over his shoulder. Far below, a speck of blood and flesh soaked clothing disappeared as onlookers swarmed around it to have a good look.

A pair of hands on each of his arms yanked him from the edge and lifted him over the railing and onto the observation deck. As the two young men in dark suits climbed over the railing, Tony recognized the middle-aged man standing in front of him; it was the bald guy.

"Who the hell are you?"

The man snickered and showed him his identification.

"We're F.B.I. Sorry I had to pepper spray you back then, but when you made me, I had no choice. It gave me an opportunity to borrow your cell phone while you cringed in the corner of the alley. I programmed a tracking device in it. That made it easier for these two young agents to keep an eye on you, although you threw them for a loop when you left your cell in your room to charge for a few days. Where did you go?"

"Cefalù, where my old friend, Todd," he pointed over the side, "lived. Which reminds me. Two questions: Why were you following me, and why did you wait so long to shoot the bastard?"

He snickered again and led Tony across the deck.

"First, more importantly, are you okay?"

"I think so. I didn't piss my pants, did I?"

"No, but most people would have. That's a long drop. Let me answer your last question. We weren't sure who the guy was or if he was armed. As soon as he pulled the firearm from his pocket we took him out."

One of the younger agents holding a phone to his ear said, "They identified the body as a Vincenzo Sagona."

"No," said Tony, "His name is Todd Kenilworth. Vincenzo is his twin brother. Todd pushed Vincenzo off this very deck last winter to fake his own suicide and hide in Italy from the mob. Todd took on Vincenzo's identity and has been living in a mansion in Cefalù."

"You can fill us in on all that later," said the bald guy. "Let me show you something and answer your other question."

He pointed toward the street that surrounded Piazza Venezia. A man and a woman, presumed F.B.I. agents, led a cuffed Laura Kenilworth-DiFoggio to the backseat of a plain, white unmarked car with a blue light flashing from within the rear window. Right behind it, two uniformed female *polizia* escorted Becky, not cuffed, into a Roman squad car. From the other side of the monument, an ambulance siren screamed.

"We were assigned to apprehend her, with the help of the Roman police, for felony charges based on evidence and testimony from the man charged with planting that bomb in your car. We lost track of her once she left Chicago for Rome. Her brother evidently helped her hide out. When we found out that you were hot on her trail, we figured the best way to find her was to tail you, and we were right. There's a guy waiting to take us down on the elevator. Let's go."

"Wait just a second, please," said Tony.

He looked down at Via del Corso, the street that led away from the Victor Emmanuel Monument. The inharmonious din of the conflicting sirens echoed and grew silent as the ambulance, squad car and unmarked vehicle sped away.

"It's finally over," he said and joined the others at the elevator.

"AT LAST"

Pauline had just begun her last set at Kingston Mines on North Halsted Street in Chicago. Kingston Mines claims the title "Chicago's Oldest and Largest Late-Night Blues Club." Tony walked inside the North Stage during the opening lyrics of the Etta James classic, "At Last:"
"At last
My love has come along
My lonely days are over
And life is like a song"
Tony loved that song. Before he had met Pauline he thought the only artist that could sing it right was Etta James herself. When he heard Pauline sing it, he added her name to that short list.

From the back of the crowd, he recalled his dream about her singing here before an all-male crowd. Sometimes reality transcends our dreams. This was a mixed gender audience. Pauline wasn't wearing a teddy, but she still looked beautiful and seductive in her short sequined black dress and heels. Unlike his unconscious vision, the crowd didn't enlarge and push him toward the exit when he approached her.

Her eyes stayed shut as she delivered the last lines:
"I found a dream that I can speak to
A dream that I can call my own
I found a thrill to press my cheek to
A thrill I've never known
You smiled and then the spell was cast
And here we are in Heaven
For you are mine at last."
When she opened her eyes, Tony stood on the dance floor just below her.

"Happy anniversary," he said and handed her the ruby and star sapphire jeweled music box.

"Oh, my god, Tony, it's beautiful," she said. Her voice amplified as she spoke into the mike, but she seemed oblivious to the crowd.

"That's not all. Open the box. I have a special request," he said.

She lifted the lid. As the tinkling melody of "Volare" began, she reached inside and extracted a shiny white-gold engagement ring with a huge sparkling diamond.

Tony dropped to one knee and said, "I did a little more shopping after I bought the music box. What do you say?"

She held her hands over her mouth, gasped, took a deep breath and said, "That's a song I sang only once before. You know it didn't work out too well."

"I sang it once, too, with bad results. But I don't think the song was bad; it was just a bad arrangement."

"I think you're right," she said as her eyes welled. "I'm willing to take the chance if you are."

The crowd gave them a standing ovation as they embraced.

EPILOGUE

August 15, 6:10 p.m.

The discord of sirens penetrates her ears and soul as she rides through the Rome city traffic with an F.B.I. agent on each side of her in the backseat. She feels no sadness, no fear, no remorse, no tears, just numbness.

In less than two decades she had lost a husband, her father, the love of her mother and possibly her daughter if she was to be convicted of three counts of conspiracy to commit murder and much more.

She looks at the date and time on her watch and has to chuckle at the irony of it. Seven months earlier, to almost the exact day and time, she had lost one brother. Minutes ago, she lost his identical twin in the same way.

"Déjà vu, Italian style," she says.

The agents glance her way and then ignore her.

ABOUT THE AUTHOR

Déjà vu, Italian Style marks **Lou Macaluso's** second installment in the Tony Morelli mystery series. Before becoming a best selling author and motivational speaker, Lou was an English teacher, football track and wrestling coach, triathlete, and a union president. He currently serves as a Mystery Writers of America Board Member.

His other published works include *In Search of Sal* (premiere Tony Morelli mystery inspired by the true story of a Hollywood character actor), *The Warmng Sicilian Son, Clown Town*, and numerous short stories. Lou currently resides with his wife and their three dogs in Chicago.

ACKNOWLEDGMENTS

No author writes alone. Just being the only living human pecking at the keyboard does not justify claim of sole authorship. In my case, Addison Clark, my canine muse, resided in my office during the creation of every phrase. But many people within my life and head contributed to the production of this book.

The artistry, editorship, and professionalism of Chris Moebs and the Pegasus Books staff breathed life into my work. My lifelong friend/business manager/literary agent Mark Garry gave me headstrong advice such as "You're old. Just do it." Marcia Trahan and Dorinda Urbauer, my personal editors, showered me with the honest and sometimes harsh, but needed criticism.

Mystery Writers of America, Midwest Mystery Writers of America, and particularly my colleague/fellow author/mentor/friend Helen Osterman provided the support, resources, and community that yield quality noir writing.

Every fictional character in this book evolved from real characters and compilations of people in my life. Hall of Fame Blues singer Nikki Armstrong and bar buddies Harry Downey, Tom Knoll, and Bob Wagner (also advised me on police procedures) inspired characters. Matt Lulich (Lulich & Goff, Attorneys At Law), Larry Anoman (Anoman & Associates), and Mark and Lee Ann Foley (Come On Inn) provided models for commercial and professional establishments.

A special thanks to these people who participated in a pre-publication campaign: Chris Hennessy, Cynthia Marshall, Cres, Schultz, Dan Mead, Dave Bond, Denean Calderone, Frank and Marlene Hench, Frank O'Lone, Fred Pearson, Jacki Hartnett, Janet Hansen, Jim Sartori, Joe Mazzeffi, John Martz, Jose Saldana, Kathleen McNeeley, Ken Yearly, Laura Kaufman, Liz Dewitt, Mona Wadington, Marcia Duncan, Mary Trost, Nancy Bagge, Pam Zychowski, Paul Loparco, Rae Ecklund, Sue O'Lone, Tom Rottmayer, Vicky Knopf, Hope Smith-Highley, Bill Brody, Carl Zambo, Eileen Evans, William Daley, Sharon O'Donnell, Sally Joseph, The Sopkos (Sheree, Mike, and Sage), Michael Henry, Joy Fox, and Carl Durnavich.

order at pegasusbooks.net

www.ingramcontent.com/pod-product-compliance
Lightning Source LLC
Chambersburg PA
CBHW050522260626
47157CB00004B/1428